THE OUTER HARBOUR

THE OUTER HARBOUR STORIES

WAYDE COMPTON

ARSENAL PULP PRESS  VANCOUVER

THE OUTER HARBOUR
Copyright © 2014 by Wayde Compton

US edition published 2015

ARSENAL PULP PRESS
Suite 202–211 East Georgia St.
Vancouver, BC V6A 1Z6
Canada
arsenalpulp.com

The publisher gratefully acknowledges the support of the Canada Council for the Arts and the British Columbia Arts Council for its publishing program, and the Government of Canada (through the Canada Book Fund) and the Government of British Columbia (through the Book Publishing Tax Credit Program) for its publishing activities.

"1360 ft³ (38.5 m³)" first appeared in *Prism international* 43:4 (Summer 2005) and *Mixed: An Anthology of Short Fiction on the Multiracial Experience* (Norton, 2006), in both cases under the title "The Non-Babylonians" and in a somewhat different form. "The Lost Island" is a response to "The Lost Island" by E. Pauline Johnson (Tekahionwake); her story, first published in *Legends of Vancouver* in 1911, is itself a reflection of a tale told to her by Chief Joe Capilano (Sa7plek). "The Instrument" first appeared in *Event* 40.1 (Spring/Summer 2011). "The Front: A Reverse-Chronological Annotated Bibliography of the Vancouver Art Movement Known as 'Rentalism,' 2011–1984" first appeared in *The Fiddlehead* 259 (Spring 2014).

Cover art: Detail, "Merapi," by Diyan Achjadi
Design by Gerilee McBride
Edited by Susan Safyan

Printed and bound in Canada

Library and Archives Canada Cataloguing in Publication:

Compton, Wayde, 1972–, author
The outer harbour : stories / Wayde Compton.

Issued in print and electronic formats.
ISBN 978-1-55152-572-3 (pbk.).—ISBN 978-1-55152-573-0 (epub)

I. Title.

PS8555.O5186O98 2014   C813'.54   C2014-904455-0

C2014-904456-9

This book is dedicated to my father,
Levi Compton Jr., 1938–2012

CONTENTS

Sometimes the house of the future is better built,
lighter and larger than all the houses of the past, so that the
image of the dream house is opposed to that of the childhood
home. Late in life, with indomitable courage, we continue to
say that we are going to do what we have not yet done: we
are going to build a house. This dream house may be merely a
dream of ownership, the embodiment of everything that
is considered convenient, comfortable, healthy, sound,
desirable, by other people. It must therefore satisfy both
pride and reason, two irreconcilable terms.

—Gaston Bachelard, *The Poetics of Space*

1,360 FT³ (38.5 M³)

━ ━ ━ ━

It is as if the apartment has become its own culture. Their lives serve the space where they keep the curtains drawn.

Home from the afterhours, the three of them collapse on the living room couch. Riel flattens out the newspaper on the coffee table and just looks at it, not even trying to actually read. Kelly puts the situation into words: We're coming down, so now what?

Phone Frances, Erika says.

Riel feels a twitch of despair. His body wants sleep. But that, he knows, will be impossible for hours yet. Another pass will delay the inevitable crash. Erika already has her phone open, is talking tersely to their fourth roommate.

While they wait for Frances to get there, Erika flicks on some cartoons and sits in front of the television. Kelly gets out her crayons and notebooks and takes up a spot at the coffee table, going for the bright colours. Riel watches her doodle inconsolably and fiercely, and he watches the blue wash of the TV's light shift across Erika's face. He totters over to the CD player and puts on some Roni Size, and Erika automatically kills the volume on the TV, her eyes never quite deviating from their fix on the animation flashing across the screen. Riel looks at Kelly and feels something near desire. She's grinding her jaw, chewing on nothing, her mouth cycling with rhythm and without sound.

By the time they hear Frances's key in the door, Riel has been on his back on the couch for an hour going through the same somatic pattern: closes his eyes, thinks of sleep, realizes his eyes are open again, staring. The girls similarly get up, sit down, get up, and look out the window over and over.

Frances breezes in. She says, How was it? Still high?

Not quite, Erika says. Her nose is running and she sniffles loudly.

Frances sits next to Riel, making him sit up. Louie Louie, she says to him loudly, setting down her infamous briefcase beside the *Chronicle*. You're looking rough.

She never calls him by his proper name, and Riel never corrects her. He can only assume, as everyone does, that he was named after the Métis revolutionary—but why, exactly, Riel does not know. His father vacated his life without ever explaining the odd christening. (He knows three things about his father: he is black, he is from San Francisco, and he is long gone.) As far as Riel knows, he has no Native ancestry, and all his mother can say about his name is that Riel's father convinced her during her pregnancy that it sounded "musical." Frances, a proud urban Cree, finds it amusing that a non-Native carries such a meaningful name for no real reason. She is polite enough not to make fun of him for it directly, but she makes her skepticism of the great man's misinvocation known by always hailing her roommate with the song "Louie Louie," sometimes even singing the Kingsmen's melody as she calls him out.

You know, Frances, I think maybe the best thing is that I just tough it out and go to sleep, he says.

Kelly blanches at the suggestion. She opens her mouth as if to speak, but just sighs in quiet agony.

No, Erika says. No. We're going to hit it *again*. Summer's almost over. When school starts, we're going to have to get straight. That means we have to do as much drugs as we can *now*. That's just how it fucking *is*.

That and you called me all the way here, Frances says. You're buying something.

We want more and so does Riel, Kelly says. She glares at him.

Frances fiddles with the combination lock on her case, covering one hand with the other to block their sight lines. Riel watches her hands for a moment, but looks across the room when she shoots him a glance. The case snaps open and she says, Okay. What do you need? I've got it all. I just saw Victoria last night.

Who's Victoria?

Not a *who*, a *where*. My connection from the island was just in town. The lab rat. I'm so hooked-up now, it isn't even funny. Up, down, and all around.

After some haggling, Frances pours out three short rails of meth onto the Roni Size CD case. Intra-urban rails at best, Riel thinks, if "rails" they are: rapid transit shit, for sure, and definitely no John A. Macdonald, CPR, continent-spanning rails. But beggars aren't choosers, and they are taking Frances's crank on credit. Ostensibly, she is responsible for a quarter of the rent, but they always chisel the payment out of her in drugs before the first of each month, an overdraft Frances keeps meticulous track of. Riel can't recall a single month of the last six that they haven't ended up owing her money rather than expecting it from her on the first.

Riel is spent, and his body is crying out for mercy and rest, but he says, What the fuck? as a kind of grace, and hoovers up the acrid powder anyway. He feels like a rag doll one minute, but three minutes later he is standing up, feverishly hunting around for more drum 'n' bass.

Summer's just about done, Kelly says wistfully, her head back to catch the nasal drip. I can't believe it's almost over. Let's walk to the beach. I want to put my feet in the ocean.

Let's do it, Erika says. She stands up, looks around at everyone, smiles and nods like a mental case.

Frances laughs. You're nuts. You've been dancing all night and it's six a.m. You're going to walk to the West End? It's like five miles away, you freaks.

Riel puts on his shoes and starts lacing them up. Kelly and Erika watch him, then do the same. They all put on their sunglasses and start for the door.

Frances, who only dips into her own supply on days of the month that are prime numbers (or so goes the myth she is known by), puts down her briefcase at the end of the couch, where Riel has just been, and lays her head upon it. Riel has seen her sleep like this many times, protecting her livelihood, he knows, from them—which only mildly offends him. He is always amazed that she can sleep with a four-cornered piece of luggage for a pillow.

They leave Frances there and go sleeplessly down the apartment stairwell, on past the intersection of Broadway and Fraser, and all the way up Main to Terminal, west to Pacific Avenue, and through Yaletown, till they finally reach Sunset

Beach. There, Riel, his girlfriend, and her best friend stand knee-deep in the greedy tide. They savour the last days of the first summer of the next one thousand years with hallucinations of motion in the peripheries of their sleep-deprived eyes. Riel turns to look and there is nothing there but that which is there. Chasing his own optic nerve. Sneaking up on a mirror.

THE NEXT DAY, Riel wakes up and extricates himself from Kelly's unconscious embrace. Erika is on the other side of her, sleeping too, still wearing her shoes. He notices there is sand and seaweed in the sheets. He sneers, gets up, scratches, stretches, and wretches twice. There's nothing in his stomach, so nothing comes up. He goes to the living room. No Frances. He looks out the window. It's sickeningly hot and bright out.

After washing up and eating four pieces of unbuttered toast and a bowl of ice cream, he looks in on the girls. They're still asleep, and he envies them, but nevertheless perches himself on the couch and picks up the newspaper he put there a day earlier. The article that attracted him returns to memory. He cradles his head in his hands and reads:

MYSTERY MIGRANT FOUND IN SHIPPING CONTAINER

VANCOUVER—Thursday, 23 August 2001—Longshoremen unloading a container ship yesterday at a Vancouver terminal were shocked to discover a single female stowaway of uncertain origin amongst the usual cargo.

While offloading a container at Centerm, workers noticed the sound of a human voice coming from inside. They immediately broke the lock, opened the container, and notified the Vancouver Police Department. The standard 20' X 8' X 8'6" container had been converted into improvised living quarters, including a portable toilet, a supply of food and water, blankets, a battery-powered lamp, and small breathing holes drilled through the walls.

The woman emerged gesturing frantically and speaking in a language none of the workers could identify. The container has been confiscated by the VPD, and the woman is currently being detained. Citizenship and Immigration officers are trying to determine her identity, which is at this time unclear.

The ship itself—the MSC *Quantus*—was last loaded at the Kwai Chung Container Port in Hong Kong.

Longshoremen interviewed on site disagreed about the woman's appearance, one saying she was "probably Asian," but another commenting that she might have been "Arabic." One worker, who is fluent in two dialects, said he did not recognize her language as Chinese.

Until her national origin can be determined, police will not comment on whether or not this is a case of human smuggling.

Riel re-reads the article, then speaks its headline aloud to himself. Wanting to know the story's development, he goes down the apartment stairs and up the street to a café, grabbing a house copy of the day's paper. He orders a cup and settles in.

Two summers earlier, hundreds of Chinese nationals arrived on the coast illegally from Fujian Province, packed onto rickety fishing vessels, and then too Riel watched a media circus develop around their incarceration and deportation. That was the same year Riel had first read *The Autobiography of Malcolm X* and *Soul on Ice*, books that had stirred and changed him.

When he noticed that everyone in his family, and everyone else he knew in Port Corbus, were angrily unanimous about wanting the refugees sent home, he saw, for the first time, a cohesion among them he had never before fathomed. Everyone in his family was white; everyone he knew in Port Corbus was white. On the issue of illegal aliens, at least, all the people in Riel's life thought alike. He developed a sympathy for the Fujian migrants. Could he help them somehow? Should he write a letter to the paper supporting them? What would El-Hajj Malik el-Shabazz do? Riel read everything he could find about racism in Port Corbus's small public library. Then he narrowed his hip-hop consumption down to only the wisest artists: The Coup, Dead Prez, and MC Kaaba. He re-evaluated his position that Bob Marley was something to do with the hippies who sold pot on Patourel Beach in the summer, and he bought every CD from *Catch a Fire* to *Confrontation*, poring over Marley's lifetime of lyrics year-to-year as if they were a singular epic.

Armed with a new political outlook, he challenged his teachers and wrote all his essays about racism. His grades improved. He cared about the essays he wrote, which counted for more than he had imagined to teachers in a resource-economy town with a high dropout rate. Riel had begun high school indifferently, but at the end was surprised to find himself accepted at his second choice of universities in the Lower Mainland. His mother and stepfather were pleased with his success, but dubious about his new stridency—which was, of course, the key to everything. That he is snorting his student loans and attending few of his classes is a turn he hadn't anticipated, a turn that his family knows nothing about. He resolves to hide this carefully when his parents come down for a visit the week after next.

But here, in the pages of the *Chronicle*, Riel finds a case of illegal immigration far more strange than those of 1999. It's now Day Two of the story, and, as he expected, the paper is all over it. The Mystery Migrant is still in custody, but surprisingly, they haven't yet determined anything about her: they can't be certain of her point of origin or even identify the language she is speaking. The authorities refuse to speculate to the media, but there are already letters and an editorial about the case. The letters are all shrill and mainly depict her as some sort of terrorist or spy: What economic refugee can afford to send herself in such relative individual comfort? One of the letters calls for her to be sent home immediately, saying "she should be stuffed back in the container they found her in, locked up, and sent to Hong Kong with 'return to sender' painted on the side." Riel chuckles darkly. They want her sent back, and they don't even know where she is from. There was no photograph in yesterday's paper, but this article is accompanied by a shot of the woman sitting in the back of a police cruiser. A streak of white—glare from the window reflecting the camera's flash—bisects her face, but Riel can still see, examining her features, why there is confusion about her race. She looks, as they say, maybe Asian, maybe Middle Eastern. It's hard to tell. Riel himself is used to being misrecognized. He traces her face in the photograph with his finger. Maybe Asian, maybe Middle Eastern. Where does one end and the other begin? There is such a thing as both, he knows.

He puts the newspaper down and finishes his coffee. As Erika pointed out, summer is nearing its end and the start of school looms. The coming semester will be make-or-break because Riel is on academic probation. The apartment, friends, clubs, and drugs have come to eclipse everything else somehow. What he loves about Kelly is how she drenches herself in bright colours and plastic accessories, like she's wearing toys rather than clothes. She is quirky, in a steely sort of way. In the apartment's kitchen she has multi-coloured refrigerator door magnets that are letters of the alphabet, and with them she's spelled out *THIS IS THE LAND OF YES* on the white surface; beneath that, Erika added *THERE IS NO SHOULD*. Together these form the apartment's own esoteric Charter of Rights and Freedoms. The scene is both cold-blooded and peace-and-love at the same time. It drew him in and turned him on. But he's fucking up school. If he flunks out, he has no alternative plan. Erika tends to shut down this sort of talk by saying: Twenty-year-olds are supposed to fuck up. That's our job. But Riel is not so sure. The girls are middle-class white kids of university-educated parents and seem sure that everything will eventually work out no matter how lost they get. Riel, however, suspects that he has just this one shot. If he fans on it, he'll be feeding timber into a table saw in Port Corbus for the rest of his life.

Riel takes the newspaper and walks back to the apartment. Inside, the girls are up and moping about, abstractedly tidying. Nobody speaks, and the three of them move as if the others aren't there, like ghosts among the living. Riel goes to his bedroom and pulls a box cutter out of his desk, slices the photograph of the Mystery Migrant out of the *Chronicle*, scratching up the hardcover of a textbook as he does it. He pins the picture to the wall above and behind his computer, next to the photo of his other hero, MC Kaaba.

To Riel, Kaaba is better than Tupac or Biggie, better than

any other rapper, though far less famous. When he first heard Kaaba's lyrics when he was fifteen, Riel was mesmerized by the strange mix of conspiracy theory, self-confession, and Koranic exegesis based on a Nation of Islam splinter group that Kaaba's parents had raised him in, the Khufu Faction. Indeed, part of what first attracted Riel to Kaaba's music was the connection he felt he had with the rapper because they both came from families belonging to weird religious minorities. Riel's mother had re-married and converted to her second husband's faith, so at age eleven Riel was baptized in his stepfather's church, the New Occidental Jerusalem Church of Christ. Riel's stepfather, Walker, had helped to found the church in Port Corbus in the 1960s with several other American draft dodgers who had come to British Columbia during the Vietnam War. (Riel's mother seemed serially attracted to American exiles.) The church had begun as a hippie-oriented, LSD-soaked affair, but over the years had boiled down to a hard core of Jesus-freaks eventually pious enough to renounce drugs and free love. Riel once read a critique of the church on the Internet that referred to it as "a hippie revision of Pentecostal evangelism, created out of expatriate nostalgia." He'd quit the church when he was sixteen.

Riel sits and stares at the two photographs, of MC Kaaba and the Mystery Migrant, side-by-side on the smoke-coloured wall, then he shifts the mouse so his computer will wake up. He opens a program and stares at its grey-framed whiteness, thinking about writing. He stares and breathes until the screen saver finally blips back on, scrolling words that he punched in seventeen months earlier. The scrolling text says to him, BY ANY MEANS NECESSARY ... GET OUT OF PORT CORBUS.

IT'S FRIDAY AND Riel has attended every class of the semester so far, though it is only the first unfruitful week. Coming home from campus, he enters the apartment and encounters Frances doling out jib to some geezer and his young boyfriend. Riel got his student loan deposited directly into his account earlier in the week, so he gets in line. But the two guys don't leave when they've scored, they make themselves at home, doing bumps off Riel's textbooks without asking. This, he recognizes, is happening more and more: he'll come home and Frances will be entertaining; there'll be a strange kid asleep in the bathtub, some pale girl rooting through the fridge for food. Riel worries that his CDs are going to get scammed this way, or his computer. But he doesn't feel like he has much to say about it because the place is really Kelly and Erika's. He moved in by default, just by crashing here so regularly. Then Frances offered to pay a quarter of the rent so she can use the place to crash or deal when she's in the neighbourhood. They presume she has another, real home somewhere else. It's users' economics: Kelly and Erika are getting thrifty, looking for ways to spend less on rent, more on drugs. He eyes the skinny hustler who is fondling his copy of *36 Chambers*. Frances produces a small vial from her "files," and she and Riel trade. He pockets the stuff for later.

I was gonna make some tea, she says, and she ambles off to the kitchen. Riel follows her and takes a seat at the kitchen table. Frances flicks on the radio while she gets the kettle going, and Riel catches the wrap-up of a radio show: a male host thanks his female guest, they exchange pleasantries, and then, in summary, the host explains that he's just interviewed the Mystery Migrant, and that what was thought to be human smuggling was in fact a hoax—some kind of art performance. The last thing the host says is that she—the artist—will be part of a panel discussion with some other artists that evening, presenting on her project. He ends by giving the time and place. Then the show moves on to some other topic.

Riel stares at the radio until the kettle whistles, then he stares into its sound.

HE CAJOLES KELLY and Erika into going to Mystery Migrant's panel by promising that they'll party hard afterward. It's dumb, Riel knows, because his parents are visiting in the morning, but it's also Friday night, and he has Frances's meth and loan money in his pocket. The girls buy theirs from Frances, who is trying to nap before the evening's work. He resolves to quit at a reasonable hour, and be ready to welcome his mother and Walker in the morning with at least a few hours of sleep behind him.

At the downtown gallery, they sit through a presentation by a guy describing a performance in which he pierced his tongue with a stainless steel sickle on the steps of City Hall; then a woman talks about her series of rush-hour "interventions" in which she rode the bus wearing a business suit made of moss and cedar bark. Finally, the Mystery Migrant is up. She explains that she had herself shipped in that container, intending to get caught. She was carrying no passport, no ID. She wanted to make sure they had no idea who she was when they found her, and her intention was to document the stories that developed about her arrival, and how expectations shaped perceptions. To add to the enigma, she memorized a sequence of phonemes from the phrase "Tower of Babel" scrambled into nonsense, and resolved to say nothing but that during questioning. The Mystery Migrant was born in Canada, she explains, making all the calls to deport her fully ironic. It was only when she spilled some water in the Citizenship and Immigration office and swore that they realized she spoke English, and the whole thing came to a screaming halt. There are some criminal charges pending, but she factored bail into the cost of the performance, and seems unconcerned about the consequences.

Kelly and Erika are half interested in the sickle guy but fidget through the rest. When the moderator starts a Q and A, Riel puts up his hand, but immediately Kelly pulls it back down again. Time to bail, she says.

He shakes her off and raises his hand again, so she mock-punches him in the arm. The girls get up while the moss and cedar suit takes someone else's question. We're going across the street to get some smokes, Erika says. We'll meet you over there.

The crowd is small, and the Q and A doesn't go long. Riel approaches the table and talks to the Mystery Migrant, or who-ever she is. It all tumbles out: For some reason, I don't know why, he says to her, this thing you've done is really important to me. Illegal migration. This performance—. Riel acutely feels the limits of his knowledge, his cramped vocabulary for talking about these thoughts; she's at least five years older than him, and more than a few ticks smarter, and he's unsure. Finally he says, I don't know if this makes sense, but I was able to leave my hometown because of the Fujian migrants.

She frowns. What do you mean?

He lets his thinking unfold slowly. I saw in them—in what happened to them—the structure of something I want to take apart.

She looks at him, considering this. Then she nods. I think I know what you mean.

They talk a little more, about school and art, and after a moment in which she seems to take him in, she says casually, Let's stay in touch, and writes down her name—Veršajna— and her number on a scrap of paper for him. He's surprised, smiles, nods, then turns to go.

Kelly is in the doorway, watching them. She looks at him, then at Veršajna, who is now talking to the sickle-tongued man.

What was that? Kelly says tightly.

It takes Riel a second before he says, Uh, you know, just to keep in touch.

Kelly stares at him. Then she looks away and crosses her arms. So you're obsessed with her, she says. That's perfect. Then she turns to go. Erika silently mouths to him, Well? Riel understands that he is supposed to chase Kelly, so he does.

ON MONDAY EVENING, Riel's parents drop him off at the apartment. Tomorrow they'll go home to Port Corbus. All weekend he managed to spend time with them away from the apartment, doing touristy things in the city, but now Riel can't avoid inviting them up for tea, though he has no idea what they'll find there.

As he comes in with his parents, Kelly and Erika are on their way out, and Riel quickly introduces them as his roommates. Frances is asleep in the living room, so he guides his mother and father into the small kitchen. He starts the kettle and rinses out some cups. While they're waiting for the water to boil, there is a knock at the door, which Frances answers, and three guys wearing black velour track suits come in. Frances peeks into the kitchen at Riel and his parents, and then leads the dark trio into the washroom, shutting the door behind them. Riel's parents exchange glances, so he explains that the guys are helping her fix the baseboard. They emerge from the washroom shortly after. The three leave, and Frances returns to the living room wordlessly. Riel's parents finally excuse themselves. They are staying with friends and have to get a good night's sleep before the long drive home.

After they're gone, Riel phones Vers^ajna. They talk about her performance, about university and illegality, and they laugh a lot. He wants to know something, but he's been similarly interrogated all his life, so he holds back as long as he can, finally wording it as, Where does your name come from?

My name?

Yeah.

Ah.

He thinks he can hear over the phone that she is smiling. I can't say, she says. I'm still performing, you see. A concept that overlaps with the last. I haven't answered that particular question, in all its variations, for a little over two years now. I'm keeping a journal of all the ways I've been asked about my race, as well as all the responses to my non-cooperation. Every single guess and speculation.

If you're going to write about what I say, then I don't think I'll say anything.

Too late.

The two of them trade words for three hours. Then he says goodbye.

As soon as he hangs up the phone, it rings.

Hello?

There is a little piece of silence. Then his stepfather's voice: I'm not going to let you break your mother's heart.

What?

You think I'm some kind of idiot? I know what's going on in that place of yours.

Where's Mum? Let me talk to her.

She's asleep. You're screwing up in school, right? You're on drugs, I'm sure.

You don't know anything.

But you are.

Riel considers hanging up, but just squeezes the phone in his hand. If you called me just to tell me a bunch of shit that you think you know, then you've achieved that. Mission accomplished. See you later.

You should come back to Port Corbus. Take some time off, straighten out.

Not happening.

There is a sound like Walker is moving the receiver from one hand to the other. He says, Be not deceived, his voice hardening. First Corinthians, remember? Evil company corrupts good morals.

Something smacks into the living room window. Riel looks up. A bird has flown into it, he supposes. He reaches over and switches off the light. Look, I'm just starting the new semester. I'm not going north now, so forget it.

There is silence, except for a bit of his stepfather's breathing on the other end, then another thump against the window, and then the click of Walker hanging up.

Riel goes to the window and looks out. Two young guys are on the sidewalk below, one of them holding a running shoe in his hand like he is going to shot-put it up at the window again. Riel unlatches and lifts the window, leans out, and shouts, What the fuck?

Yo, is the Indian chick home? This the spot? Your line was busy, yo.

Riel scowls at them. She's out. He scribbles her cell phone digits on the pad beside the phone and tears the page out, spans his arm out into the air, and lets the note fall. One of the tweakers reaches up for it with both hands, looking, Riel thinks, somewhat like Willem Dafoe in *Platoon* when he gets blasted to shit by the Vietnamese. The little piece of paper floats down erratically, and Riel feels for a moment like Galileo dropping a feather to measure the velocity of plummeting bodies in motion. Or whatever the fuck it was he did to make the church burn him at the stake. Or was that Joan of Arc?

RIEL IS DREAMING of birds. He is watching them each land on the leaves of an enormous red tree, each taking a place on a single leaf, and the sun is behind the tree, shining through the leaves. A figure in gold is driving an axe into the base of the tree over and over, but the birds will not fly. Inside the dream, Riel can see a close-up image of one birdless leaf, the sun causing it to glow red. The axe makes a terrible knocking noise, and then Riel sees that he is looking at the sun through the inside of his eyelids. There is a shift. He opens his eyes to the light of morning. There is knocking, real knocking—the sound of knuckles on wood. Muffled shouting. His name being called. Kelly is beside him. Who the hell is that? she says, squinting and stretching.

Riel gets out of the bed and sits at the edge. There is more knocking and someone is shouting out there. Okay! he croaks back. He gathers himself and walks to the front door.

He is reaching for the doorknob when he hears the voice on the other side.

Open up! You're coming with us, Riel! We know exactly what's going on in this apartment! Get up and get your things! We're driving back to Port Corbus, and you're coming with us!

He steps back, as if the door has suddenly burst into flames. There is no peephole in it, but he pictures Walker's blowsy face on the other side nevertheless.

Open the door! I know what's going on here! This is a place of sin!

Riel puts the heel of his hand to his forehead. Fuck off! Take your preachy bullshit and just fuck off!

Kelly, Erika, and Frances, awakened by all the noise, congregate in the hallway. That your dad? asks Kelly, but she doesn't wait for an answer. She leaves for the kitchen, and puts on the kettle. Erika goes to the living room. Frances wanders around groggily, like she's searching for something.

Stepfather and stepson argue through the closed door.

Drunkenness, revelling, and such like: they which do such things shall not inherit the kingdom of God!

Behold, a beam is in thine own eye, you fucking hippy redneck!

Oh my God, Erika says. She's sitting on the living room floor with the TV going. Oh my God, you've got to look at this.

Open up! You think it's heaven now, but there'll be weeping and wailing and gnashing of teeth later!

Frances is beside Riel now, no longer searching. Where's my case?

Your case?

Walker starts kicking the door on the other side.

Frances grabs Riel's arm. My *stash*. Where's my fucking *stash*?

There'll be weeping—

How am I supposed to know? You sleep on it, don't you?

—and wailing—

It's gone. You saw the combo on my case. I *saw* you see it.

—and gnashing of teeth!

Riel steps backward and through the bathroom door, closing and locking it in front of him. Immediately, Frances begins pounding on *that* door, and cussing him out through it. It is almost syncopated, her pounding and Walker's kicking beyond on the landing.

Riel sits on the edge of the bathtub and puts his head in his hands. Frances is shouting about having brothers who've done time in Matsqui, brothers she is going to phone who will come down here and kick his head in. Then she's quiet for a bit. Now she and Kelly are arguing. He faintly hears Walker's preaching two doors removed, but he can no longer discern the words.

Riel looks at the bathroom window. It's wide open. Outside, it's a rainless Tuesday morning. He looks out, then leans out, and observes the alley below. He climbs out the window feet first and lets himself drop onto the blacktop. Frances's briefcase is on the ground down there, leaning against the wall, ripped open, and empty. He looks up at the window, then at the case, then down the alley. He's wearing sweatpants and a T-shirt, no shoes. He starts walking.

He circles around to Fraser Street. It is just slipping into the after rush-hour lull. A half-block away, in front of the apartment, he spots Walker's parked SUV and his mother sitting inside it. He's too far away to gauge the expression on her face. She's rubbing her forehead. Maybe she's brushing her hair.

He crosses the street. The corner market, where he sometimes shops, is open and empty. Tameem lets Riel use the phone for free and asks why he has no shoes, pointing down at his feet. Riel shrugs. How else can I be sure that the ground is really there? Tameem frowns and returns his attention to his small portable radio. Voices speak of attacks on New York and Washington. While the phone is ringing, Riel asks, Attacks? But then Veršajna picks up on the other end.

Outside, he takes a seat at the bus stop and waits. He watches his mother in the SUV half a block up, unaware of him as she stares ahead. When the bus comes, Riel tells the driver that he has no money because he has been robbed. He points at his bare feet. They even took my shoes, he says. The sloe-eyed driver shrugs. Such a morning, he allows heavily in a type of English that gently rolls its r's. Riel takes a seat in the back.

On his way to Veršajna's, he decides he is free. He is commuting to the future. He imagines he will not recover his things from the apartment. He imagines he will not complete the semester. He imagines he will neither return nor repent nor weep nor wail. It is the end of everything. *Fin de siècle. Das Ende der Geschichte. Eppur si muove.* Riel speaks out loud there in the back of the bus, but the driver guns it just as he opens his mouth. The engine sounds so that none of the dozen strangers sitting and standing around him can make out his words. There is no manifest reason to repeat.

THE LOST ISLAND

⊂⊃ ⊂⊃ ⊂⊃ ⊂⊃

1

Xonotlite. Tuya. Phreatomagmatic. Anhedral. Halite. Felsic. Anhydrite. Lapilli. Pahoehoe. Hyaloclastite. Phillipsite. Rhyolite. Sideromelane. Kipuka. Phenocrysts. Scoria. Maar. Chabazite.

Jean has seen it. It's been there, above those waves, for a year and a half now. It's a natural miracle for the way it rose up out of the sea burning and sending skyward a fountain of dry ash from the mouth of the inlet. But the island is nothing personal until the morning she is reading the *Sun* and drinking tea, and Fletcher, her roommate, tosses an essay on top of the paper, blotting out its field of words with his.

Look, he says.

The pages are warm and smell like toner, freshly poured forth from Fletcher's printer. He sits down and stares at her. She realizes he is waiting for her to read it right now.

The essay is a solid block of geological jargon, and after two paragraphs she stops and skims. When even her skimming mires, she looks up at him and asks, Why are you showing me this?

I want to go there, Fletcher says.

Where?

There.

Jean looks at the essay. They've turned it into a protected zone, a national site for research, she points out. Nobody can go there but scientists.

Indian land, he says. Brand new land. Brand new colonization.

Fletcher makes a gesture toward the kitchen window. He says, It's worth some kind of intervention, occupation. Throw a monkey wrench in the data collection. Get in on the anti-colonial ground floor, like.

She looks back at the essay. Hyaloclastite breccia. Opaque petrology. Co-ignimbrite plumes. The language sits there and stares back. The language of dirt. A hundred fancy words for dirt. Flaming dirt rising up out of the dirt spewing a mist of dirt all over the settled dirt. It is impossible for her not to think of the Bible, impossible for her not to think of clay, impossible for her not to think of a few huffs of breath and how that's us— impossible for her not to think of how colonized her thinking is. Ground floor to glass ceiling.

FLETCHER IS FROM Victoria, was adopted by whites, had a Snohomish mother from the US, and a local father from a band unknown to Fletcher or anyone else who might tell him. He's never met any of his blood relatives. Jean, on the other hand, is pretty much black.

At the first meeting, a copy of a book called *Surtsey: Iceland's Newest Island*, with a photograph of an erupting volcano on the front, sits in the middle on the coffee table. Jean focuses on it during the planning.

I'm not Native, Jean says, planting her non-sequitur in the air. Everyone turns to look at her, but nobody says anything. I don't know if I should be here, she says. I mean, I figure I should say that right now. Should I be here?

Fletcher rolls his eyes.

Let me get this straight, Rob says to Fletcher, ignoring Jean. You want us to get in a little inflatable boat and go out to an active volcano in the middle of the salt chuck?

The French did it. There. Fletcher points at the book. Journalists put a dinghy on *that* just a few days after it emerged, while it was still exploding on the other side. Then they claimed the island, half joking. Completely pissed off Iceland. But the cone on ours is barely active now. It's very doable.

Alison says, *Should* we do it, though?

Jean stares at Marc's uncrossed arms. He has a tattoo on the inside of his left forearm. Marc told her that he inked the image himself. The outline of a wing, raggedly drawn. Blue-green, freehanded. She imagines the pose required to hold a needle with one hand and draw steadily upon your own arm—to hold yourself in front of yourself like you would cradle a clipboard. She realizes the shaking evident in the image is the pain that looped between the art of one arm and the mark-making other.

FLETCHER, JEAN, AND Rob study all they can of the island— books and news articles. They fill their home with words about that half-kilometre hill of ash just this side of the line between the Strait of Georgia and the Burrard Inlet. Fletcher muses that they are studying the history of the place: a country with a less-than two-year timeline. Its ancient past was under the ocean, Fletcher muses, under the ocean floor even, sloshing around in the core of the Earth. A midden of magma, he says.

They know that earlier, when Pauline Johnson Island first bubbled up out of the water, West Vancouver, often in the path of the prevailing winds, was carpeted with hot ash, and whole neighbourhoods had to be evacuated. A day later, when the winds shifted, the same happened to Point Grey. Then Bowen Island got its turn. There was no telling at first how large the volcano would get or how long it would continue erupting. Volcanologists observed it at careful distances as it blasted ejecta into the sky. Parliament declared the island a restricted ecological reserve, and named it after the Mohawk poet who had chosen Vancouver as her adopted home.

When the island coughs up its vapours, Fletcher jokingly says to Jean and Rob, it is speaking Mohawk.

After its first harrowing weeks above sea level, the volcano settled to a simmer. It is still technically erupting, but now only produces a slow series of wispy, grey exhalations. The residents of the shores of the Strait and the Outer Harbour cautiously returned, swept up, shovelled away the thick layer of tephra that coated everything they owned, and carried on.

The little island is droplet-like. Its shape seems strangely unnatural, as if it had been designed rather than born, but scientists point out that tidal erosion will quickly re-sculpt its shorelines. Barring future eruptions, erosion might destroy the island altogether in a matter of years, they say. Nevertheless, the surface is already showing signs of plant and animal "col-onization"—their word—is already becoming a part of the living systems of the coast.

Sooner or later, Fletcher says, a pop can will wash up on its shores and it will be officially globalized. On the grid, he says.

They are neither scientists nor sailors nor strategists. Just students. But they borrow a Zodiac and buy a flare gun.

For Jean there is within this crazy plan a kind of retort to the Vancouver she has known: the school teacher, whom she loved, who one day out of nowhere called her a golliwog; all the where-are-you-froms and all the where-are-you-real-ly-froms; being looked at or looked through, depending, but being summed up, appraised, pre-emptively estranged. The plan they had was not books, not theories, but action, risk, transmutation, a half-suicidal whirlwind, something worth eruption. Something to capsize for.

Fletcher, beyond the mundane planning, seems inordi-nately obsessed with the technical composition of the island. He is learning the jargon, acquiring the lingo. Jean gets about half of what he's saying when he speaks the language of palagonitization and wind drift, allochthons and ferry wash. Fletcher almost preaches the Latin and Greek words, the sci-ence words, from the pages of the books he's borrowed from the library, reading aloud to Jean and Rob. Fletcher is high on geology.

But there's also the moment he's on the porch with her, night, wind, rain, the herbal tea he clings to, and he says, Words have to live outside as much as in, I think. Like chil-dren. If all your words are inside, their meanings will only go so far. Words need the air and weather to make things develop.

The language nevertheless makes its way into Jean's dreams, which are more and more about Pauline Johnson Island. In these dreams, she transforms into some class of life in the island's ecological succession. She is seagrass. She is bracken fern. She is thimbleberry. She's a starfish rotating in the untouched shallows, near, but not of, the rippled land, circling around and around it. At first, to her, as she and Fletcher and Rob and Alison and Marc plan, the beasts are only beasts and the plants are only plants. But now they are *flora* and *fauna*, a chain of creatures spreading north and south and east and west from all shores. A dandelion seed under the feathers of a gull. A pregnant spider in the deep dry knot of a driftwood branch. When Fletcher tells her that they call seeds that drift over on the wind "diaspores," she makes him show her the book that says this. She re-reads the sentence five times over.

She can't think of a single person related to her by blood who knows how to swim.

THEY KEEP A photograph of the island on their refrigerator door, a picture torn out of *Maclean's*. When Alison and Rob are out on the back porch smoking, Dara, their four-year-old daughter, points at it and asks Jean, What's that?

It's an island in the inlet.

In what?

Jean takes Dara by the hand to the living room, opens the atlas, and shows her. We're here, Jean says. It's there.

Dara looks at the map and then up at Jean. The child's eyes seem to darken as she thinks.

That's the inlet, Jean says, tracing it with her finger, and that's the island. It doesn't matter what they call these, though. They're yours, whatever names they use. This new island is yours. You've never had it, but we're going to give it back to you, Jean says.

WHILE THEY ARE waiting for the summer, Fletcher takes Jean to the Museum of Anthropology at UBC on a fair day. But they don't go in. He takes her behind it, to the site of the old Point Grey Battery, where guns waited for a Japanese invasion that never came seventy years earlier. High ground. They look across the water toward the island, a small grey hump on the surface of the ocean. She sees a wisp of steam marking it like a flag, though the volcano's cone is supposed to be inactive this week.

Another day they drive out to Lighthouse Park, on the opposite side of the inlet, and look from there. They are a little further from the island on this side, but again the antenna of smoke ascending from its centre is there. When it's time to go, she looks back and over her shoulder at Point Grey, where they were before. She imagines a resonance, an etch of her presence in the view from the previous week, a spiritual echo from across the body of water. A premature ghost of herself.

Fletcher clasps her shoulder and points to the open sea, so she looks. He smiles, his eyes behind his sunglasses, and he says to Jean, That container ship there? It's probably full of fucking televisions. Televisions on the water. Thousands of miles, yeah? You'd think teleportation machines existed until you really think about a thing like that. They talk about myths. A pile of rectangles on my ocean. That's the real fucking myth.

Jean watches the ship crawl across the flat blue until she sees what Fletcher sees.

THEY WAIT FOR summer, for a long stretch of easy weather and warmth. Watery calm. Fletcher is studying boating books. But he doesn't think it will be necessary to do a practice run. The presence of the island has killed a lot of the shipping traffic, so he thinks it'll be simple. Rob likes to break the tension by messing with him, calling him Skipper. Or sometimes just Skip. When they're arguing, they call him Captain Vancouver. Sometimes they even call him Captain Bligh.

Most of the arguing is over the communiqué. At one meeting, Fletcher presents a long essay to the group, which he calls a draft, and he invites their intervention. But when the four of them start picking apart what he has written, correcting phrases and altering the wording, Fletcher shouts until he gets his way.

Nevertheless, at the next meeting he's entered the changes, giving them each a copy of the document titled "Liberation of the New Pan-Indigenous Territory."

Jean turns the word *symmetry* over and over in her mind until it sounds wrong, made-up, fabricated. Symmetry. Starfish. Symmetry. Sand dollars. Symmetry. Asymmetrical resistance. Fractals of bodies made out of bodies and carrying forth the bodies of the past.

SHE CAN'T TELL whether or not they are together. They are planning and spending a lot of time with each other. But she's not sure what *all* it is, what more it might be.

Fletcher was bounced around a lot as a kid, Alison says when Jean asks. House to house, foster homes. I know a bit about that myself. There's a quiet part to him. I don't know what's there.

Dara interrupts, asks if she can be taken to the park. Alison tells her to go put on her shoes and the kid sprints for the front hall.

Whatever it is you're going to get from him, Alison says, you're probably getting it now.

Jean's feelings hover.

2

Chiasmata. Synapomorphy. Mitosis. Clade. Chromatid. Uracil. Allele. Plasmid. Haplotype. Diploid. Nucleotide. Cline. Meiosis. Interkinesis. Holophyly. Thymine.

Three months later, in the summer, on the Zodiac with Fletcher at the helm, on the sun-glazed water, Jean feels the first real rush of panic. They are navigating out of False Creek, with a hull full of minimal gear: a flat of bottled water, their rolled-up banner, a canary-yellow Grundig hand-crank radio. She doesn't fear the police, to whom they'll eventually surrender, as much as she does the ocean, now that they are actually skipping across its mask-like surface.

Rob and Alison are sitting together in the middle of the boat, shouting through the noise of the motor at each other. Marc sits back with the gear, lounging in his seat with his shirt off, as if he's on vacation.

Jean catches Alison's eyes. Her fear, she's sure, is apparent. Alison breaks off her argument with Rob.

We were just arguing about a spelling mistake, Alison says. A typo. That's all. Alison holds up her phone, the only one they've brought, and she says, I just sent the communiqué off. It's done. We'll be there soon. Relax.

Jean nods and picks up the yellow shortwave. Hugs it to her chest like it could be eased.

THE LOW SLOPE on the horizon is there, but the thin tower of smoke that plumes upward and leans slightly in their direction is what finally holds their attention. The sight quiets them all. The island's emanations are minimal, and have remained unchanged for quite some time, but still, the suggestion of fire causes them to turn mentally inward.

What's the correct verb, she wonders: *land, beach, disembark*? Whatever it is they'll do, she thinks, they'll do it upon an earthly fuse.

THE ISLAND AIR seems to shift between cold and warm. Jean wonders if what she feels is only the heat of her imagination or if the island is venting. Standing there, on the solid ground, she feels a sudden pulse of nausea, and she coughs until everything in her stomach comes up and out on the ash.

Waited till you were on dry land to be seasick, Marc says.

Alison watches her, goes to her side, pats her back while Jean's bent double.

Afterward, Jean buries her bile with a few kicks, covering it with the island's moonlike dust.

JEAN LOOKS TOWARD the centre, at the spire of smoke coming out of the cone. It's steadily rising, but there's no lava. No danger that she can see. But being this close to the smoke itself, a few city blocks distance, is alarming. They gather their matériel together—their tents, the cooler, and the banner—and march through the tephra. By the time they are seated at the top of the little slope, their clothes are powdered with grey. The air smells like sulphur and saltwater. It's humid, but every few moments, as the breeze shifts, the wind flanks Jean and turns oven-dry. She is inside an elixir, a potion in the form of territory.

The point now is to wait for the communiqué to work its way through the channels of reportage and security, all the way to where they are, to the place that makes them illegal by being there—standing, walking, waiting, thinking, peopling it. Being people where they shouldn't be. Waiting for time to bring them in.

THEY EXPECT HELICOPTERS eventually, and each of them at different times steals a furtive look into the sky, at the eastern horizon, in the direction of the city. Police helicopters. News helicopters. The former will come to take them away, the latter to take their images from here to put on screens everywhere else. That's how big the plan is, how expansive, yet how small.

Their banner reads UNCEDED NATIVE LAND. Red spray paint on Fletcher's repurposed bed sheet. A couple poles. Holes so the wind doesn't belly it, lift it, set it sailing.

JEAN NOTICES A pocked boulder the size of a newspaper box that rests half buried in the ash several metres down the shore. It occurs to her that at some point, months earlier, that great chunk of stone flew out of the volcano and landed there. It is painted over with white bird shit, she sees, but there are no sea-birds on the island. She spots a gull out there above the water, but it just glides past. Passes them up like it knows something.

The column of smoke is in the centre, like an axis, at this moment leaning nowhere.

ALISON TAKES A piece of paper out of her back pocket and unfolds it. Dara drew this, she says, holding it with both hands. Jean looks at the crayon drawing of the island and notices that Dara has drawn six human figures on the beach. She's got them all in different shades of brown and gold, under a cream-coloured sun. Dara has put herself there, alongside them on the island, the smallest of the smiling stick-people, though Jean knows she is with Alison's mom.

Alison finishes drinking from her plastic water bottle and tips it upside down, draining out the last drops. She kneels down and scoops aside some of the ashy ground, digs out a hole. She re-folds Dara's drawing, then rolls it into a scroll and slips it into the container. She caps it and drops the bottle in the hole, covers it over. Maybe one of those scientists will come across it, she says, smiling. My girl will end up in the Museum of Anthropology. Authentic First Nations glyphs from one of the lesser coastal islands.

Jean laughs, and then she tells Alison.

THE BEAT OF the surf intensifies, or maybe Jean has just noticed it. It's crashing faster, even though the tide is receding. She looks to the shoreline, but turning her head makes her dizzy, nauseous. It's either her sickness or the sound, but something is bending, then she realizes that what she's hearing is not the tide but the thrum of blades.

On the horizon they can now clearly see the shapes of two boats and a helicopter above, closing in from the east. The chopper's windscreen is lit by rays of orange.

The helicopter moves ferociously fast. They can only stand and watch it.

It flies over them. Terrifyingly low. They all instinctively dive to the ground, lie on their bellies as it roars past. A rain of paper comes down upon them.

Leaflets. The same text over and over. It begins: HOW TO SURRENDER.

THEY TURN ON the radio. Not a word about them yet.

Then Alison's cell phone goes off.

They are all quiet as she takes it out and looks at it until it stops. Then it rings again.

She throws it into the surf, sidearm. It skips beautifully three times.

THE ARGUMENT:

It's so far been all police, all the boats and aircraft. They have obviously grounded the media. The island's relative inaccessibility is the cause of this flaw in their plan. No media, no point. They must at least rate a single photograph.

Fletcher says they need time. Someone will break through, some telephoto lens will bust the cordon and get their image. It's inevitable. Cops can't police the whole ocean. You can practically windsurf your way here. They need to buy time.

They need to delay the takedown that is on its way.

But no one is sure how to do it.

Fletcher stares at the ground. He says to it, Right.

HE'S AROUND THE other side of the cone, scanning the sea and sky. The chopper is gone for now, but the two boats float out there, not yet moving in. Fletcher walks further along the beach, across from one of the vessels. The others watch him as he shuffles around down the shore.

He's limping, Jean thinks. He's dragging the toe of his combat boot through the littoral ash, turning here and there. It's like he's gliding across a ballroom floor. Soft shoe or Indian-style, she can't decide. Either. Both.

Or he's cracking up.

Later, on the mainland, after, she will see on a screen a photograph that will by then be famous, impossibly taken from a bird's-eye point of view. Jean will read in the picture the lie Fletcher wrote in the sand, to keep the law away.

WE ARE ARMED.

The island's first dance.

THE CORDON BREAKS. News helicopters and all manner of boats. The cops come alive. The occupiers only now see multiple figures on the decks out there. The blue and white helicopter is on its way, they know, purely by the feeling of unleashing that surrounds them.

3

Pele's hair. Limu o Pele. Pele's seaweed. Pele's tears.

Jean goes to Fletcher. There's not much time, so she takes his hand, puts it on her belly, and says it all: a new life, theirs; she didn't say before because she wanted to be here, and the group might not have let her come.

Blades beat apart the air, and ash rises around the five. They stand and look up at the helicopter and hear a voice from a loudhailer command them to stand apart, to turn around, to put their hands behind their heads, to fall to their knees, to put one ankle over the other, to remain motionless. They don't. The sound of the chopper is deafening as it hovers. The men with the weapons rappel down and storm toward them, through a blizzard of ash. When she feels the barrel of the AR-15 jab into her sternum, she hears Fletcher shout, No! She's on the ground, a knee on her spine, ash in her eyes, and the sound of shouting, the blades breaking the sky, and a rush or a whoosh or an exhalation. A change in the space around her. Is the island erupting? It's only in memory, later, that she hears the blast. An explosion, in her recollection, audibly vaster than it can really have been. She re-hears the gunfire in the cochlea of her mind, the sound that takes him. She can't see anything, but feels her wrists being zip-tied, then her whole body being netted in something, the force of a man moving her body against her will. Then she is rising. She is in some kind of harness, and it's lifting from the ground, then she is moving through the air. She forces open her eyes and through a blur she can distinguish the island's outline, its shore, an appendage of dust leaning out from the beach she was standing on a moment ago. The ocean is blindingly brilliant, and though her wrists and her ankles burn from their bindings, she's flying, she's moving over the face of the water like a fragment of an explosion broken free of its form.

THE INSTRUMENT

━━ ━━ ━━ ━━

Albert spots Donald at the door. Another him. But shabbier clothes. Why? It doesn't take money to not look rumpled. The way Donald walks. He wonders if that's the exact shape he cuts, too, when he moves, how he's seen. Albert watches him walk across the restaurant floor, weaving between the tables.

Hey.

Hey.

Donald's looking around for the server. Raises his hand. Albert waits until he gets his own drink going, then waits some more. It's Donald who asked him here.

That hat, Donald says, pointing at Albert's head. Who does it remind me of?

Albert knows what he means. Uncle Hayward wore these, he says.

Donald runs a hand over his own scalp, seems to catch himself doing it, puts his palm down flat on the white table. That's it, he says.

Albert and his brother only ever met their uncle Hayward—their father's older brother—once, when he visited Vancouver for Expo '86 with his wife and kids. He came up from

Sacramento, where he and their father are from. All Albert remembers about Uncle Hayward, Aunt Inez, and their cousins is the way their black American accents sounded thicker than his dad's, and that they all shared a similar physiognomy, though he and Donald had something Nordic and etiolated jumbled into it. This was, of course, back when Albert and Donald were still conjoined. Albert remembers thinking that if he could run, he would look just like his cousin Clint when he did it: skinny legs, long strides.

Donald pulls an envelope out of his pocket and tosses it across the table.

Albert picks it up. Inside it is a letter from some kind of agency. Money for Donald's film project. Albert says, Jesus Christ.

Donald smiles, touches his scalp again. That'll be enough to throw something together. Not feature-length. Under an hour. I'm gonna take some time off and just concentrate on doing this thing. It's not a lot, but it's enough.

Albert swirls his drink around in his glass, holding the acceptance letter in his other hand. He fans himself with it and says, I guess I'm supposed to say Congratulations.

You guess, Donald says back at him.

It's going to be about Dad.

About Dad, yeah, and about us. About you and me too.

Albert shakes his head. His mind is full of rage. He tries to imagine something past the anger, something more useful and helpful. He starts speaking slowly, to get it right.

Don, you go ahead and make your movie, then. But if you interview me, don't edit me. Put in exactly what I say to you, 'cause I will tell you exactly what I think. I don't believe in this, so if you let me say that I don't even believe in it, I guess you can put me in, but I'm asking you not to edit me. And I'm asking you to think twice.

Donald answers quickly. I've already thought about it, but okay. Say what you think you have to say, that's just fine. He looks at Albert, like he's assessing him. Then he reaches over and takes the fedora off of Albert's head. Albert does not flinch. Stays firm, neither scowls nor smiles. Donald puts the hat on his own head and pouts exaggeratedly, pulls the brim down over his eyes and lifts his chin.

You think you're clever, Albert says to his twin.

It's a phrase their mother used to say, joshing their father when he talked crazy. Albert hears himself using his mother's words. He thinks of the way his mother's voice sounded when she said it, the theremin-like quiver that had always been there in her tone when she formed those words: You think you're clever, or Don't try and be clever. At some point years back, Albert realizes now, the phrase dropped out of the dialogue between his parents. He can't recall exactly when, because how do you remember a trailing-off?

DONALD IS SETTING up the tripod in the middle of his living room. His father is speaking.

Is Albert going to do the music with you?

What music?

For your film.

Oh. I thought I'd do it myself. It's been hard enough just getting him to let me interview him.

Donald's father reaches over to his son's brick-and-board

shelf and pulls a book out, glances at the cover, and puts it back the wrong way around, its spine to the wall. You bought all this stuff with that grant? He gestures at the camera that Donald is clicking into place atop the tripod.

Yup.

His father nods. It's a ways to go, he says.

What's a ways to go?

We're a ways to go from the surface of the almighty God.

Just hang on, Dad. Let me get you miked.

We're a ways to go from the everlasting light of Jesus. Within the space of equations.

I know, I know. Just hang on a second. Lift up your shirt, I'm going to thread the cord through there. He raises his father's denim shirt, puts the tiny microphone up it, and reaches down with his left hand to pull it through, then he fastens the alligator clip onto his collar. Okay, I'm just going to test my levels. Donald lifts the headphones from his neck and puts them on his ears. Go, say something.

I'm having a hard time understanding why they gave you all that money, really. I mean, I'm not saying you aren't talented, because you are, both of you. You have talent. But it's a lot of money. Money can be a gift from the devil. But money makes possible the flight of the spheres. The Wright brothers believed the world was square. I may ask to borrow some of that money, Don, but I don't want to take anything away from your art, so maybe you'll just wait until you think the time is right.

Donald takes the headphones off and looks at his father. Sure, Dad, I'll give you some of the money. Absolutely I will. But listen, man: the levels are good. So just hold on a second. See this here? When I start rolling, this light will go red. Then

I'm going to ask you some questions. And you just say your thing, okay?

I copy that.

Donald presses RECORD. We're rolling. So, tell me, you were talking a minute ago about God. What does God mean to you?

Why's the light red?

What?

The light. Why's it red?

You mean the light on the camera?

Yes.

It's red because it's recording.

Yes. But why *that* colour? Why is that the recording colour?

Donald shrugs behind the machinery. I don't know. Why do you think red is the colour of recording?

I don't know.

Donald presses PAUSE. Dad, what I'm doing here is making a documentary about you. Now I know you have a lot to say about a lot of things. Right? This is your chance. It's possible that a lot of people might see this. So it's your chance to set the record straight on whatever you feel like talking about.

I was just asking you about the light on the camera. You want to be a filmmaker, but you never thought about that. I find that puzzling.

Well, maybe it's puzzling, Dad, but nevertheless it's not really what the film is going to be about. It's supposed to be about you. So let's talk about you.

The only discussion worth our breath is the discussion of how we're supposed to enter the kingdom of God when we have no understanding of the notion of infrared.

There you go, Donald says. He hits RECORD once more.

The light is on again, his father says, squinting at it. I have to say that the thing I'm thinking is that the best performances I've ever seen were the ones they failed to record. I saw Roland Kirk one time in San Francisco, before you and your brother were born, and your mother and I were seated next to this college student with a camera. His machine was running all through the show, and by the end of the show he opened it and realized that the whole thing was messed up. Someone had put the wrong size film in it or something and it was all chewed up. He was beside himself. Like a child pitching a tantrum. Roland Kirk had brought the house down, and all this college kid could think about was some chewed-up tape.

I see. Okay. You made a few jazz records back then.

I did. Uh-huh.

Do you want to tell me about them?

No. You've heard them. Just learning then.

What did you learn from making them?

I learned that I'd rather do what I do now.

Which is?

I'm a carpenter. Semi-retired.

Do you like doing carpentry?

I cannot ask for more. I'm happy.

Donald lifts his head and looks at the ceiling. He puts his hands on his hips and closes his eyes. Then he presses PAUSE on the camcorder. Let's quit for now. Okay, Dad? We'll do this another day.

There may be no more days. The moon does equations and the sun does equations. But it's not a showdown between them, it's no duel. Because each and every star does its own equations. And those stars that have planets, those planets do equations. And those planets that have moons, the moons do their own equations. It's a slide rule the size of God's thigh bone.

Okay, Dad. Donald moves from the equipment and lies down on his couch, facing away from his father.

May I disentangle myself from this machine now, Don?

Yeah, man. Disentangle yourself. Maybe we can try it again later.

Donald's father unclips the mike and unlaces himself. You were born with God's creativity in the tips of your fingers, he says.

There's a sixer of beer in the fridge. Grab one and get me one, Dad, if you don't mind, and we'll watch TV, okay?

It will watch us, Donald's father says.

He goes to the kitchen and returns with two brown bottles.

ALBERT CHOOSES TO wear the fedora during the interview. He'd considered sunglasses, but thought that'd be too much.

The red light is on.

Tell me about yourself, Donald says from behind the camera.

Where should I start?

Tell us what you do, how you make a living. Or how you wish you made a living.

Well, I teach music, privately. I'm a tutor. I teach kids how to play guitar. How to read. And I play, of course. You and I had some minor success years ago, toured around the country, got on the CBC, recorded some stuff that went nowhere.

Are you bitter about that, the fact that we went nowhere, as you say?

Albert rolls his shoulders. Readjusts himself. Bitter? No. Just real. Those were good times, but I'm fine with just gigging around town here with my little group. The Albert Abbey Trio. He centres his gaze on the camera and says, exaggerating his voice like a stentorian radio announcer, Last Saturday of every month at Lambeau's in Gastown. He lifts his look beyond the frame, to Donald. You don't mind if I get a plug in, do you?

No, fine. So what's the difference between what you do now and what we did when we played together? I mean, how do you feel about the direction your music has taken?

Albert clears his throat. We were reacting to a lot of things. That's how I think of it now. We were trying to break out of a kind of expectation. It's quite ridiculous, really. But it was a personal reaction to our environment. I mean, have you explained our condition, in the film? Like, how are you narrating this? Are you going to voice it over?

I'm just interviewing people so far. You tell it.

Okay. Albert leans forward in the chair and focuses on the camera. Donald and I were born craniopagic. Conjoined at the top of the skull. Totally rare. Rare to even get born, and then very rare that we would live afterward. They say there's no more than a dozen people like that at any given moment living and breathing on the planet, that's it. And we weren't considered safely operable at first because we shared the artery that brings blood to your brain. We didn't actually share very much brain matter—it was that artery they were worried about. So Mom and Dad were advised to let us be. But science caught up with us eventually. Now, this is going to sound like a digression, this next part, but bear with me for a second. Okay, our father was a musician, a kind of minor jazz musician before he came up to

Vancouver in the seventies, before we were born. And he taught us both how to play music, how to read music. And we really took to it. The doctors were tickled about that. They saw it as therapy, I think, us doing something involving motor skills. But Dad would have taught us to play whether we'd been conjoined or not. You know what I mean?

I think so too. Go on.

Well, we weren't half bad, really. And we formed a band when we were still in high school. Got our buddy Paul Mack to play drums. He was great. I think you should always get a drummer who has ADD, you know? It seems to be maybe the one place in the world where that is an advantage. Anyway, the thing that messed with everybody's minds was that we were playing punk rock. Like, three-chord punk. Really simple power-chord crap. The stupidest, easiest shit. I played guitar and you played bass. See, but you were too good, really, and that was the problem. I still think you're the reason we didn't actually get listened to as punk. It wasn't just the freak factor. This is a criticism and a compliment, so don't make that face. Physically, of course, you *could* play like Dee Dee Ramone, but psychologically you couldn't *let* yourself do it. Because you were just too capable, basically. You filled everything in, all those little runs. You were bored. I am probably guilty of that too, so don't make faces at me, seriously. We sounded like D.O.A. infiltrated by James Jamerson, and it was just a mess. Not a *punk rock* mess, just a *mess*. But that doesn't matter. What I'm saying doesn't make all that much sense because, truthfully, we were just a story on the news: two freak twins play in a band. We couldn't *help* but get on TV. But that was the problem. We were news rather than music. Nobody was ever going to listen to our sound no matter what we did.

We were rebelling against Dad, you think, with the punk thing.

Of course. Dad was all Ornette Coleman and Sun Ra, so we chose the dumbest, most regressive three-chord form. I don't know. It's not a unique story, if you put aside the craniopagy.

So talk about the surgery. From your view, what did that do?

To my music?

Sure. Or whatever.

This is the ironic thing. Is it ironic? I don't know. But anyway, it was because of those records Dad cut in the sixties. That's how the surgery happened. Like I was saying, Dad was in this little quartet in San Francisco, and they did three records back then with some little outfit called Clairvoyance Records. They sunk like a stone, and then Dad became an acid casualty, married Mom, moved up here.

"Acid casualty". That's a harsh way to put it.

Let's just say that Dad lives in a permanent state of improvisation these days. Does that sound better?

You were talking about our operation.

This guy in the States, this Silicon Valley, nouveau riche multi-zillionaire heard about us—on the news, of course. He's a complete jazz fanatic. White guy originally from San Francisco. He saw the story about us, but recognized Dad from those old records back in the day. He was a fan, a collector, the type who tracks down every last recording from an artist, who wants to own it all, every bit of it. And he had always wondered what had become of Dad after those three records. He's a software guy—David Lloyd is his name, I should really thank him here, because he was very generous to us. He tracked Dad down and actually flew to Vancouver to meet us all. I imagine you'll use that picture of us for this movie, Don, the one where we're all at that restaurant?

I will. Go on.

He meets us. We all hang out. Everything's fine. It seems like Dad must have held his tongue or something, because Lloyd was charmed. Then he flies back to California and pretty soon we get a letter saying he's arranged things with this super-surgeon. The long and short of it is, he flew us down to California and paid for our operation, and it went perfectly. They had a team of fifty-eight people working on our operation. I will never forget that number. Because, back then, I used to imagine all fifty-eight of them crowded around the operating table, elbowing and shoving each other to get at us, but obviously it wasn't like they were all in the room at the same time. Anyway, so today *this*—Albert lifts his hat and bows his head toward the camera—is all that I have left of my seventeen years attached to you, bro.

Donald zooms in on the oval of pale scar tissue that marks Albert's otherwise sepia crown.

Albert settles the hat back on his head and cocks it a little, leans back in the chair. We are free of each other because Dad made a few mediocre hard-bop LPs in 1969.

Do you really think they were mediocre?

Those are Dad's own words. But you're right, he's hard on himself. It was a beginning, but he never got further than that, because—well, maybe he should tell his own story. See, I don't even know if you know this, but Mom told me that the whole time during the lead-up to our operation, Dad was trying to get Lloyd to put up some money for another record.

Yeah, I know.

Here's the thing: Mom says Dad made a demo recording for Lloyd. He played it for him, and the guy just stopped taking his calls. And this is *before* our operation, mind you. Mom was freaking out, trying to keep Dad from screwing it up. She thought he'd scare Lloyd away before they went through with separating us.

Where's the demo?

Dad gave it to Lloyd.

What was it called, did she say?

"Jesus Defines the Surface of the Caul."

Surface of the Call?

That's *caul*, as in c-a-u-l.

Donald scratches his eyebrow and sighs. So if I asked you to describe the music you do now, how would you describe it?

Jazz. Not punk. Serious business. I play with a bassist who thinks Mingus is God and a drummer who thinks keeping time is for sell-outs. Dad won. I'm halfway to being him. All I have to do is go mad and I'll be all the way there.

DONALD IS IN the passenger seat of his mother's Corolla. It's just after her shift, and she's taking them through Stanley Park and across the Lions Gate Bridge to her North Shore condo. Up on the bridge, which arches over and above the inlet, it occurs to Donald that they are not only seeing the view, they are a part of the view. They are being the view.

I'm sorry, his mother says, but I think I agree with Al on this. I mean, I can see why you'd want to do it, and I'm happy that you are expressing this creative interest, but I don't know. I'm concerned.

About what?

She licks her lips, changes lanes. Well, what is it that you want to ask me?

About everything. Anything. What it was like raising two kids like us. What it was like when we were on TV and in the newspapers. Stuff about Dad. Whatever you want to talk about.

I don't know what I have to say. If you want to read all the newspaper articles I have about you, I have a closet full of them, whole albums full of clippings. You can go through all that if you want to. But I don't know what I have to add to it.

Do you have any clippings about Dad?

Well, he's mentioned in a couple of the news articles, after David Lloyd got in touch with us.

Anything from before that, on his music?

She cocks her head for a second, sort of shaking it, sort of shrugging. We met just after he was quitting music. You've heard the whole story before.

But didn't he make a demo tape for David Lloyd, when they were getting ready to operate on us?

She looks at her son, then returns her attention to the road. Yes, he did.

Do you have it?

She purses her lips. Then she shakes her head. He gave it to Lloyd. Or at least that's what he told me he did.

Mom, can I turn the video recorder on?

What, right now?

Yeah.

Why?

This is interesting.

Oh God, do you have to?

Can I? He leans over and unzips the backpack at his feet.

No, no. I mean, really, what's the point?

What was the demo like?

Are you going to turn that thing on? Won't the sound be awful in here?

It's okay.

Why don't we wait until we get home?

The car has begun the low, sloping descent off the bridge, and Donald's mother rides the brake as they go down the ramp.

What was the demo like? Did Dad play it for you?

She shakes her head again. Not the whole thing. I only heard a bit of it. Just enough to know that it was a bad idea to give it to Lloyd.

Why? What was it like?

She slows the car and it curves around the off-ramp. She clears her throat as she gears down.

Donald, you know that your father is not well. He was an immensely talented person. When I first met him, he would play the clarinet for me, and it was like diamonds—I don't know how to say it, like rays of light. But, you know, I also loved just watching him take the instrument apart and clean it. That was almost as beautiful, seeing him take it apart, look at the mechanisms, study how they worked. That's the thing; when I met him, he loved the music, but he was talking about *making* instruments, not playing them. He wanted to quit playing music. It was a different time. There was this tension between being free and drifting around, which is what we sort of wanted to do, and the discipline of being in a band. I guess he resented the regularity, the time the band took up. And those

guys didn't like me. Because I was white. They never said anything to me directly, but there was a feeling that they thought I
was this white girl taking him away from his music, which was
totally untrue. Your father, when I first met him, was already
talking about quitting and moving away from San Francisco.
Honestly, I think part of what attracted him to me was that I
was Canadian. I think he had an idea to go away with me to
Canada right from the get-go, when we first met, like I was
there to take him away from the States. You see, when we left
to live in that commune in Oregon, it was *his* idea. They were
my friends, yes, but it was his idea to go there. He wanted to
become a carpenter, he said, and make musical instruments
in his spare time. The commune was a total disaster, of course,
and we moved up here afterward. You and your brother were
conceived at the commune, though. Is that too much to tell
you? That was the only good thing to come out of that experience. Anyway, we moved up here and prepared to raise a
family. By the time he became an immigrant to Canada, your
father had really turned his back on being a musician. And
that's when all the Jesus stuff started creeping into his thinking. Not at the commune. Here.

And the demo?

His mother steers the car east along Marine Drive.

He hadn't been making music for years by the time David
Lloyd came around. He taught music to you two, but that was
the extent of it. You remember. He had no interest in it himself,
other than to teach you two. But when Lloyd came around, I
think he flattered your father so much that he got the idea back
into his head. So he built this floor in the garage, a false floor.
I don't know how to describe it. He built this rickety sort of

wooden floor, like a floor with gaps between the planks. And he did this kind of dance or series of steps around the floor, and it would creak.

I remember that. Dad laid a floor in the garage. Are you saying he built a tap-dancing floor? Donald looks away from his mother and out at the road. He told me and Al it was just a floor, just to cover up the cement.

No, he had designed it specifically to creak—that's how he described it. He claimed he had designed it to creak in patterns when he walked on it in certain ways, and that by standing and swaying and walking around on this floor, he was making a sort of music out of the creaking. He insisted to Lloyd that this was a kind of free jazz, you see. And he made a reel-to-reel tape of it after he was finished. I watched him try it out. He was swaying around and staggering, it looked like, but with the utmost concentration. I couldn't bear to watch him do it. He played the tape for me. I didn't need to hear that either. A bunch of creaking wood sounds. I didn't want Lloyd to hear it because I thought he would figure out that your father was not so lucid, and it might break the spell, his idolization of your father. I was fighting to get you kids separated, so that you could have normal lives. But how can you stop your father when he gets an idea into his head? He sent the tape to Lloyd anyway. But David Lloyd was a decent man, I believe. He must have realized what was going on, because after that point he only communicated with me regarding your operation. I don't think he gave your father any sort of answer about the tape. Your father was gravely disappointed. He had expected Lloyd to produce his new record—this creaking floorboard music. I waited until after you and Albert were separated from each other, and then I separated from your father. But maybe this is telling: the fight that we had, the one that made me decide to leave him, was about David Lloyd. Your father hated him for ignoring his demo. *Hated* him. Despised him so much it overcame any gratitude for what the man did for you two. Your father's eccentricities had always seemed benign to me, up to that point. That was the first time I thought that he seemed totally to miss our interests as a family—and your health and happiness—because of his delusions. In retrospect, I don't know if it's so bad, but at the time it was the excuse I used to leave him. I love him, we all love him, and we'll be friends until the day we die, but I just had to get myself outside of his head, you know? We're home.

She wheels the car into her driveway.

The recorder is on Donald's lap, the lens aimed at the inside of the car door, but the microphone is on. So he's gotten it all.

In the living room, his mother spreads the contents of an old suitcase onto the coffee table and they sort through the archive of his and his brother's conjoinment. Donald picks up a clipping printed on yellowing newsprint and looks at a photograph of his own young grinning face. In the picture, his head is tilted to accommodate the pull of his brother's body beside him, part of him. Donald cannot now recall the moment or even the day when the photograph was taken, though he recognizes the background as their family home in East Vancouver. In the photo, his smile is wide and he's looking directly into the camera. Albert, beside him, his head, neck, and body making the other half of their arc, looks away. The image of his brother's body has been cropped—has been halved—by the frame.

ALBERT STEPS OUT of the key of C and into A, while Michael walks the bass line in circles and Werner punctuates the departure with some skittering rim work. Lambeau's is a supper club, so Albert can only go so far outside—he has to be careful not to completely alienate the tourists and foodies and couples on dates. But he's familiar with this edge, and knows just how many liberties he can afford to take per set. He hunches over his Gibson, balanced atop his bar stool on the little stage. His fingers and his mind move apart and together. He is levitating in all directions, outwardly and inwardly.

Donald, with the camcorder cradled on his shoulder, snakes in and amongst the trio, focusing an extreme close-up on Michael's fret board for a moment, then moving on to film the bell of Werner's ride cymbal. Then he closes in on Albert's pick guard, tightening on his right-hand work. Donald squats in front of his brother, placing the camera up close to the guitar's body, the lens just a few centimetres from Albert's right hand.

Albert leans back and pulls a note north, like a man hiking a catamaran against the wind. He's aware of his brother down there near his feet, but he shuts his eyes, pursues the sound.

Donald tries to stand up out of his squat, holding the shot, but he's unsteady on the balls of his feet. He loses his balance and tips forward. The eye of the camcorder touches Albert's knee, then Donald rights himself into a crouch and backs away.

Albert keeps tinkering in A, reaching for the crow. That's what their father taught them to call improvisation. When they were kids, the old man said to them that musicians are magicians, pleasers, entertainers. What you do is no different from sawing a woman in half or making a coin vanish.

But Albert and Donald's father also told them there is a maze that the music makes, and there are moments when you are a magician reaching into your top hat for the rabbit you hid there earlier, and instead of a rabbit you pull out a crow. The trick tricks you. That's what the best music is: you reach for the crow when you know there's nothing but a rabbit in there. Yes, it's only a supper club, and Albert is only running through old standards for distracted tourists. But Albert is reaching for the crow nevertheless. It takes a kind of non-concentration. A kind of self-obliteration. And there is his brother, a frigging camcorder all up in his face, all up in his conjuring. Rabbit. No crow. Just rabbit.

Albert scribbles out a few more notes in A, then looks up and over at Michael, signals for the chorus, and goes there. Michael catches it and follows, but cocks his head as if to say, What's wrong? Werner halts altogether, but quickly punts with a strong crash, and finds them on the one.

As the chorus drags forward, a freckling of red appears on Albert's white pick guard. Several droplets of blood spray against the plastic during his crab-like picking. A woman in the audience says, Oh my God. A few people point. Albert brings the song home quickly. When it's over, he holds up his ring finger and examines it in the spotlight. He turns it toward the audience, to show them, then he shows it to Michael, who just stands there shaking his head. Werner shrugs and starts to unscrew his cymbals. Donald zooms the camera out, steps down backward off the stage, panning the trio now.

Albert leans toward his microphone: I'm sorry, folks, it looks like I cut my finger. I'm very sorry, but we'll have to stop the show. I hope you enjoyed it, and I hope we'll see you again. He turns the volume down on his Gibson and unplugs it. There is a little applause.

Michael taps him on the shoulder. What the fuck?

Albert ignores him and looks instead at Donald. He says, Shut the camera off.

No, I want to get this.

Shut it off or I swear to God I'll snatch it out of your hands.

Donald lowers the camera. What's your problem?

Werner comes around the drums and the four of them stand in a cluster on the stage. The sound man puts a CD on, and the room fills with pre-recorded contemporary.

Albert makes a grab for his brother's camera, but Donald pulls it back just in time. All right! He hugs the camcorder to his chest, away from Albert. Look, I'm pressing STOP, you fucking psycho.

Albert points his finger in his brother's face, so that the tip is just beneath Donald's nose, and he says, That's it. That's all the footage you'll get of me. Then he takes his guitar and leaps over the monitor, walks through the kitchen doors, and is gone.

Donald is left there with the band. What the hell was that?

Werner looks at Donald and says, It was the last footage you'll get of him, apparently.

Michael kicks Albert's stool, sending it clattering to the floor. He curses loudly and drags his Engelhardt off the stage by its dark neck.

DONALD IS ROLLING.

Sounds like he juiced, Donald's father says. He's seated in his son's easy chair, his hands clasped across his diaphragm.

I can feel the heat from those lights, Don. Can you dim them down?

They're to get rid of the shadows, Dad. They're necessary. If you're hot, take off your cardigan, 'cause I can't open the window either. The sound outside.

I can abide.

Donald is behind his camcorder, which is now a little bit mutilated. He gouged the red light out with a screwdriver because the lack of it seems to loosen his father's tongue.

What do you mean, juiced?

Well, it sounds to me like Al did not want to continue performing. So he juiced. He cut his finger on purpose.

What?

That's an old trick. Keep a little piece of razor or an old tin can lid or whatever stuck in your instrument. Jam it in somewhere you won't likely touch it by mistake, but somewhere in plain sight. So whenever you want a show to stop early—joop—slice!—you're free, contract or not. No one can expect you to play if you've got an injury. Some guys used to sew razor blades up under the inside of their lapels, so if some fool grabbed you that way, he'd pull back a handful of his own blood.

How come I never heard of this juicing thing? You never told me about that.

Should I have told you about that?

Well, how did Al know about it, if it's an old-school thing?

The blood has a way of talking, has a way of talking you into letting it get to where it's going.

Donald frowns. But I don't get what Al was so upset about, why he got so huffy.

The blood will escape. It has its will. It is the will of God, the blood. The blood of Jesus and the wine of the sound. Water into will, blood will out. Jesus walked on blood, turned water into wandering.

Did you ever juice, back when you were playing?

Wars have been fought over whether wine becomes blood inside of yourself or not.

You're talking about transubstantiation? Yes, I guess that's true. There have been wars about that. But I asked you if you ever juiced back when you were playing in your band.

I am juicing now. We are juicing over and over, now and forever, Don.

THE TWO BROTHERS are facing each other across the threshold of Donald's apartment.

You gonna let me in?

Dad's coming. I'm interviewing him. I'd rather you weren't here for it.

That's exactly *why* I'm here, Albert says. His lip is curled. He points at his brother's chest, stabs his index finger in the air as he talks. You're done with this project. You're going to give me the camera and I'm going to stomp it into dust. That's what's going to happen.

Donald doesn't move. Am I supposed to be scared of you? Dad's gonna be here any minute, and we're doing this interview, so step the fuck off.

But Albert shoves his way past Donald, slamming the door behind him. He marches into the centre of the living room, to where the camera is set up on its tripod, reaches for it.

Donald dashes to intercept his brother. Body checks him before Albert can put his hands on the machine and sends him crashing into the bookshelf, but they both manage to stay on their feet. Donald has Albert by the shoulders, has him pinned against the books, which are falling to the floor as they fight.

You're not going to put him on screen, Albert shouts. You either agree to quit or I will fuck up your camera. Either way, you're done.

Donald's weight is pressed into his brother to keep him from moving. All I'm doing is letting him talk. Letting you and Mom talk, too. Asking some questions. That's all.

Albert rakes at Donald's hands, trying to release their grip on his jacket, but there's no budging him.

You're exploiting him. Disrespecting him. It's bullshit. He's fucking mentally ill and you're using that to make a film.

Do you ever listen to what he says? There's something there. Something I've never heard anywhere else.

I don't give a shit! And you know what? I looked it up. I know what's going on.

Donald scowls, keeps pressing in. What are you talking about?

The money you got, Albert says. I looked it up, the fucking grant you got. That's a David Lloyd charity. Lloyd is bankrolling you to make a film about Dad. What the hell is that?

Donald lets go of Albert. He takes a step back. He just looks at his brother.

Albert steps away from the shelf. Straightens his jacket. Breathes heavily. Spits on the floor. Says, That's right. Got nothing to say about that, do you?

He's a fan. So what? He takes Dad's work seriously. Takes his life seriously. Donald gestures at the camera. And who better to make this film than me? I'm not ashamed of him. You're the one who's disrespecting him by trying to hide him away.

Lloyd has no business fucking around with our lives. Who does this, following some random family around? Who constantly intervenes in people's lives like this? It's bizarre. And you know what? The show is over. Albert swats at the camera, sends it to the floor. A crash. Pieces skitter across the hardwood.

Donald reaches over Albert's shoulder and tries to pull him down into a headlock, but Albert squirms free. Hunched low, Albert goes at Donald's legs, throws his arms around them, and takes him down hard. Donald tries to get up and over Albert, tries to get his weight above his brother, but Albert has splayed his legs out, his toes to the floor, while he hugs Donald's thighs. Donald brings his knees up and breaks Albert's clinch, then takes him by the lapels and tries to flip him over, his hands wound into the cloth of his brother's jacket.

They are holding each other, pulling and pushing, grabbing, shoving. The same weight, the same reach. Breathing heavily. One gets a burst of energy, moves the other a little, tires. The other does the same, loses strength, stalls. Isometric. Trench warfare. They embrace each other angrily, panting, on the floor. An anatomical echo. The familiar proximity.

Then out there, on the other side of the door, a snap. A creak. A creaking.

They both look at the closed door. It stays closed. They listen.

A squeak. A complaint of wood against wood. A shuffle. Another shuffle. A wail and a pop. A squeaking glissando. The pressure of someone's weight shifting on the floor in the hall.

They look at the shadow of two feet in the gap between the

door and floor. They hold on. Sit there while he performs on the other side.

A creak. A creaking. A slow cracking. Then his feet on the floor walking away. And his muffled voice. We gave it up. It gave us up. You had a path of cosmic heights between you. Through the artery. That's the tunnel where the thinking would flow. One man dreams of swimming and the other man kicks his feet. One man floats on water and another man prays to God. This is the way it is, the two of you, together. To suture. In tune. To the—

Unintelligible. The sound of the stairwell door opening. The closing of it.

They sit there for a while, entwined, quiet. They listen and listen. But their father is gone.

They look at each other. Stare. Their breath is caught.

They both think, See?

THE FRONT:

A Reverse-Chronological Annotated Bibliography of the Vancouver Art Movement Known as "Rentalism," 2011–1984

━ ━ ━ ━

Mølbach, Henley. "After the Box: Has the Cassette Swan Script Collective Killed Rentalism?" *The John Pembrey Lee Appreciation Society Newsletter* 2.4 (Summer 2011): 4–9. [article with interview excerpts]

In this piece, Mølbach (who is, apparently, the sole hand behind this irregular newsletter) summarizes the controversy associated with the decision by the Cassette Swan Script Collective (CSSC) to feature a donation box in their 1268 Commercial Drive, February 2011 front. Citing debates on the *RentalismVancouver.moc* message boards, as well as personal anecdotes, Mølbach traces a potentially factionalizing split in opinion between hard-line purists and those who believe that the growth of the movement depends upon donation collection. Mølbach explains the gist of the former group's argument—that it evinces a passionate adherence to the original model set by Everything Must Go (EMG) and their maxim, "Nothing's for sale, but you're free to browse." Essentially, the article points out the obvious by saying that a principled anti-commercialism forms the core of the Rentalist concept. The pro-donation-collection voice is, Mølbach asserts, the minority opinion within the movement, and she points out that there is no hope of donation boxes ever turning an actual profit; at best they will make it easier for collectives to run a greater number of fronts.

To expand on this, Mølbach interviews the CSSC themselves. She begins the interview portion of the article by asking the CSSCers (who, in the tradition of Rentalist anonymity, use pseudonyms; in this case, "Aisle Zero" and "Unworker") if they can verify a story circulating both on the message boards and by word of mouth that a disgruntled Rentalist expropriated the donation box at the 1268 Commercial Drive front and started distributing the contents to patrons as well as passersby on the sidewalk outside. The CSSCers insist that this story is false but say that they don't mind the development of such urban myths as an extension of the debate. Mølbach then asks them (rather boldly) how much money they made, but the CSSC decline to give it up, describing the take only as "negligible" and "not even close to breaking even." They do, however, acknowledge that whatever money they made will offset some of the difficulties the members have had in raising funds for future fronts. Unworker's answer to the question of whether or not the collection of donations was worth it, in light of the controversy and division it has caused in the movement, is worth quoting at length for the position it articulates. He says:

> It's a conversation that has to be had. In a way, it's not even about the money. It's about the growth of the form. It's about whether or not it can continue at all. In a way, for us, it sucks because it's like when they called Bob Dylan a Judas for playing electric instead of acoustic. I'm not comparing us to Bob Dylan, but what I'm saying is that when that happened to him, people thought going electric was this huge taboo, and that it would kill folk music, it was the end of the world. But he was just evolving as an artist. In retrospect, it isn't such a big deal. Forms evolve. Things transform. We want Rentalism to be around long enough that we even have a history to speak of. It's not us who's killing the movement. It's people who don't want it to change who are going to kill it.

Mølbach points out the curiousness of Unworker's statement, arguing that, from some points of view, the folk music revival *was* killed by Dylan's conversion to electrical amplification, or by some larger set of circumstances including it. (She also tries to sort out, to no helpful effect, the comparison of Dylan's lyric-centred music with the fact that most Rentalist soundtracks are closest to instrumental "post-rock.") At any rate, Mølbach ends the article by editorializing on the origins of the movement and the speculation that the EMG, the original Rentalists, either had a wealthy patron or were themselves rich enough to fund their projects independently, despite their assertions that they slept on the floors of their fronts and spent the first years of the movement virtually homeless for their art. In the end, Mølbach suggests that whether or not the anti-consumerism of the original concept is undermined by the presence of passive solicitation, the controversy is as much a formal issue as it is political. Ultimately, her argument is that the donation box intrudes upon the dream-logic of the Rentalist form. Its presence is basically a spoiler.

The Storefront Liberation Front. *Our Manifesto*. Vancouver: New Curtain Press, 2011. [pamphlet]

In this essay, the SFLF explain their particular position on the Rentalist movement in the usual, expected ways: They are careful to pay respects to Lee and the EMG, and they root the form in the concept of the *flâneur* and so forth. Despite the deadpan tone, at least some of this is probably meant to be satirical. For example, the SFLF describe the Situationists as "proto-Rentalists." But the political orientation that this position paper reveals seems sincere—even, one might say, overly earnest. The collective asserts that their members are a mix of anarchists and libertarian Marxists. And they make much of the idea that Rentalism's use of commercial space for anti-commercial purposes is subversive, and all the more so for the fact that the movement was born in the most expensive property market in Canada. However, the SFLF also express their hope that the form will spread to the United States in the wake of the global financial crisis. But there's no analysis of why Rentalism seems unable to budge from its city of origin, half a decade after its birth. At any rate, the *Manifesto* is typical until it gets to its twenty-one (!) terse and enigmatic appendices. The best of these begins with a quotation from R. Murray Schafer's *Voices of Tyranny: Temples of Silence*:

> Shattered glass is a trauma everyone is anxious to avoid. "He shall rule them with a rod and shatter them like crockery," is a potent acoustic image in Revelation (2:27). A keynote of the Middle-Eastern soundscape under normal circumstances, crockery became a violent signal when broken. For us the same is true of glass. And yet one cannot help feeling that the mind-body split of the Western world will only be healed when some of the glass in which we have sheathed our lives is shattered, allowing us again to inhabit a world in which all the senses interact instead of being ranked in opposition.

To this, the SFLF add,

> In Vancouver, the so-called City of Glass, how can we not cheer on Schafer and his urge to crack every last antiseptic condo tower window, coating the sidewalks with so much shining rime? Everyone hates the rioters, but we say the only thing hockey is useful for is showing people that they don't have to submit to life inside a town that resembles a snow globe. And during the anti-Olympics demonstration in 2010, when that masked protestor smashed the Hudson's Bay Company window, did he not teach us the absurdity of paying billions of dollars in security to protect thousands of dollars worth of glass? But

what about you, Gentle Reader? Don't have the guts to smash shit up? Then do what we do: Make anti-capitalist windows. The SFLF says: Let those who smash, smash. Let those who are not so brave instead hack the very concept of the store, the very concept of shopping. Free the consumer, if only for a moment, from the sociopathy of the work-shop-buy-despair-work-shop-buy-despair chain of behaviour that underpins the neoliberal nightmare. Rentalism is the smash-and-grab turned inside out.

A later appendix compares the function of the Rentalist front to past modes of music audition—to the phonograph and head-phones—and, more interestingly, to lesser discussed media, such as the old record store listening booths and the car radio, each in their own ways encased in this reviled-but-ubiquitous glass.

YBIYBI. Liner notes. *A Moth in a Bagpipe*. Scintillatrix Media Formations, 2009. [booklet with compact disc]

The acronym for this collective almost certainly stands for the old retailer's warning "You break it, you buy it," though this is never explicitly stated anywhere in the text. The name of the collective is made more significant by the fact that this document, which accompanied the third front opened by the YBIYBI group (1450 Venables Street, June 2008), was the first to actually distribute a physical product to patrons. Embedded within the various trips that the YBIYBI had set up in this front was the instruction, "Ask for your complimentary CD from the proprietor." This message was placed in such a way that it could only be accessed after a series of trips had been executed and most of the soundtrack had been un-muted. If patrons asked, they were given a CD of the entire soundtrack, which was packaged in a jewel case and came with this booklet. For the movement, this was a first in two ways: Never before had a hardcopy of the music been given out at a front, and the liner notes eschew the Rentalist convention of anonymity by featuring the names of the musicians, published alongside the instruments they played on the soundtrack (which, more conventionally, has no lyrics, but rather ethereal, non-linguistic vocals, by either a female or falsetto male singer called "P. Hagood"). Because the disc itself is credited to the YBIYBI group, one assumes that the musicians are members of the collective—yet the musicians cited come from a few different local independent bands, which some people on the message boards have suggested means they were merely hired to play and/or write the composition for the YBIYBI, who concentrated fully on the design of the front. YBIYBI itself has not responded to this, to my knowledge, and the email address for the group in the liner notes bounces back. In addition to the accreditation, a very brief statement is printed in the booklet, which I quote in full here:

> This disc is not for sale. It exists under anti-copyright and may be distributed, sampled, re-mixed, uploaded, and plagiarized in any non-commercial manner you wish. But if you try to make money off it, the YBIYBI collective will personally hunt you down and kill you. We mean it.

The cover of the booklet features a tartan moth against an abstract geometrical background involving multiple circles. The music is composed of emotive guitars, bass, drums, tympanis—and a Hammond organ at the middle eight. The production is well-aerated and sparse, building up to some fine wall-of-sound crescendos. In EMG fashion, the music is looped even here on the disc, and the track repeats three times. Each four-minute cycle has been seamlessly mixed together in post-production.

Compton, Wayde. "The Reader." 2009. [unpublished short fiction]

The founding myth is well-known: The EMG credit the author John Pembrey Lee's obscure 1984 short story "Cassette Swan Script" as the origins of the Rentalist concept. In it, Lee features something vaguely like a Rentalist front, though the EMG actually coined the term themselves and iterated the form as an actual art practice. The EMG have claimed that they happened upon the story by chance, and fixated on it because it reflected something they had already been considering, though in a less clearly articulated way. At any rate, because Lee appears only as an enigmatic footnote in the small body of Rentalist writing, I followed the research trail, which led me to Compton, whose academic work has concentrated on black writers in British Columbia. Compton (who knew nothing about the Rentalist connection to Lee's work) eventually showed me his as-yet unpublished story "The Reader," and patiently answered my questions about it, insisting that this story (and the story of how it came to be written) encompasses most of what he knows about Lee.

While "The Reader" is ostensibly fiction, important elements of it are provably factual. Compton uses himself as the narrator-character in the story, and Lee also appears as himself in the text. I'll summarize the plot here.

The narrator (Compton) is given a long-lost chapbook called *Reference to Resonance*, self-published by Lee thirty years earlier. He's never heard of Lee before but is so impressed by this long poem that he is compelled to track Lee down, simply to meet the man behind the book. Lee is, however, a recluse, and Compton must follow a series of contacts from Lee's past in order to locate him in his hermit-like bower in rural northern British Columbia. Compton finds Lee's camp when the man is out and ends up reading a story he finds strewn about the floor of Lee's tent. When Lee returns, however, it becomes clear that the reclusive writer has renounced all his past work. While Compton implores him to publish the scattered manuscript he's found there, Lee refuses, explaining that it is part of a project he calls "The Conflagration Files." Essentially, Lee's new "practice" is that he immediately destroys whatever writing he completes, casting the pages into the fire as soon as he is satisfied that the work is indeed finished. Lee tells Compton that he has burnt six books this way so far over the past two decades, and that the manuscript Compton holds in his hands throughout this conversation is the next to be torched. Lee senses that Compton is considering taking the manuscript with him, with or without Lee's consent, but rather than trying to stop him, Lee merely asserts that he wants to burn the pages—he calls the process "immolative publication"—but that he won't stop

Compton from doing whatever he will. Then Lee exits while Compton is distracted. After agonizing over the decision, Compton reluctantly burns the manuscript in the fire and returns to Vancouver. (One notes, however, that a version of the burnt tale appears in the story itself when it is summarized during the scene in which Compton finds it at the camp.)

So how does this touch upon Rentalism? Only obliquely, thematically. In Compton's story, Lee's disinterest in publishing subtly suggests the same anti-consumerist impulse captured in "Cassette Swan Script." But that appears to be the only connection.

Did any of the events of this story actually happen? In my correspondence with Compton in 2011, he provided the following answer:

> "The Reader" is fiction. John Pembrey Lee did publish a wonderful chapbook called *Resonance to Reference* (I reversed the title in my story) in the 1980s and it's true that I did travel to Prince George to meet the man. Lee doesn't, however, live in the woods in a tent, nor does he burn his writing as a matter of course. He lives in a house in PG with his wife. He's not really a recluse either, though he likes his privacy. My story's origins are hard to describe, but to give you an idea, a couple days after I met John we ended up doing hallucinogenic mushrooms together, at his urging. He kept saying to me that he did writing workshops, and he wanted me to participate, so we did this thing. He made psilocybin tea, and I paid him eighty bucks to take me through a series of actions I can only describe as psychodrama. This was off in the woods in a

camp similar to the one I describe in the story. Inspired by this "workshop," I drafted out what eventually became "The Reader" when I got back to Vancouver.

Compton leaves off saying, "If I had to put a number to it, I would say it's four-fifths fictional." Note that the payment of money to Lee for his workshop seems out of step with the anti-consumerist theme suggested in the story itself. In response to this discrepancy, Compton wrote, "Oh, I paid him the money. That part is definitely true." And when I asked him if Lee was aware of Rentalism itself, Compton said it never came up during their conversations, but then Compton himself was unaware of it at the time, and so did not ask Lee about it. For further clarification, I've repeatedly asked Compton to put me in touch with Lee directly, either by phone, mail, or email, but he so far has ignored my requests. None of the conventional ways of looking for Lee have turned up anything either. Whether or not Lee is a recluse, it's easy to see how that interpretation has been applied to the blank space he cuts in the public realm.

Susini, Teresa. "But Is It Commerce? Down the Rabbit Hole with Vancouver's Maverick Art Collective 'Everything Must Go.'" *Cascadia Subduction Zone* 17.8 (August 2009): 9–10. [Interview]

This is the only print interview with the EMG. Susini asks them about their latest front, which turned out to be their last. There is some detailed description of the logic behind the location site,

906 Main Street. Most intriguingly, however, Susini spends a good amount of time discussing the collective's very first front, the one that started the Rentalist phenomenon, and gets them to comment on how it expanded from their own private joke into an actual movement. Emma G. suggests that when they created the Gastown Front (on Water Street), they worked by feel rather than plan, using Lee's short story as a kind of sketch. She says that when the SFLF appeared a few months after with their own front (on East Hastings), the EMG was delighted and encouraging, and that they soon realized they ran in similar social circles, were friends of friends. What's curious about this interview, though, is that Vice Versa and Lou Leir get several details about the front wrong. For example, I personally recall the furniture as being almost all fold-out chairs rather than a mix of chairs and couches, as they imply here, and the water cooler trip (which un-muted a vibraphone-type track, if I remember right) was indeed functioning, though they say it was not—I pulled myself a cup of water from it, so I know I'm right about this point. What Susini does elicit from the EMG is their sense of nostalgia for the early days of the form. They confirm that it was Versa and Leir themselves who sat as proprietors at all hours, one or the other. I remember Versa hunched over the desk, doodling, her dark hair sweeping the page while her arm worked to create ephemera. She wouldn't look up, most of the time, answering all my mystified queries with the now-famous (and used to the point of cliché) statement: "Nothing's for sale, but you're free to browse." I spent most of a morning there, and then came back every day of the next week, examining this and that—a lamp, the hard cover books on a shelf, the calendar hanging on the wall, each of

which would or would not trip a device causing another layer of the sound track to come spilling out of the hidden speakers, a song we would later learn was called "Against Summer."

At that first front I had fallen not through a rabbit hole, as Susini puts it, but into a dream. I think it was Orwell who wrote about the first time he ever saw a motion picture at a theatre in London, saying that it was like dreaming while awake, but like dreaming someone else's dream. A mix of confusion, irritation, and wonderment that gives way to a strange pleasure—*that* was the feeling. You get there once, inside that sensation, and you seek it out again and again, to go back to that disappearance of the self, that sighing sense of annihilation and dissolution. The first time is a surprise, and you can never completely suspend the anticipation again, but that doesn't mean it's ruined. You go there again as though you are new, as though you know nothing, and you believe it, that you're lost, because the room that looks so normal and banal—like a junk shop or a waiting room—has the power to break and re-make you completely.

_____, _____. "Rentalism: The Story of the Front." 2007.
   [unpublished essay]

This one's mine. I tried to get it published at a few different places: the local dailies and weeklies. No bites. I thought of putting it up on the web. Might still do that. But it's quite out of date now. There were only the three groups working at that point: EMG, YBIYBI, and Out of the Rain, so the more visual aspects were yet to come. Out of the Rain, I am told, paid particular attention to space as image, but I missed their front, for personal reasons, and that turned out to be the only one they ever did (439 West Hastings Street, April 2007).

To summarize: I describe the form, as it was at the time—a reaction against the de-materialization of contemporary popular music. The Manichean split of music completely shorn of any object presence. The new generation, I argue, does not necessarily take this in stride, adapting to the music-as-mere-information-file future without sticking up for the thing-ness of sound. Is it the tenacious longevity of DJ culture that keeps the flag of materiality flying? We are supposed to believe that the young are free of sentimental attachment to obsolete tools, that with the invention of each new media platform there is a Khmer Rouge-like resetting to Year Zero, a cold clear re-education about the trash that is the past. But it ain't necessarily so. Was the best legacy of hip-hop the adamantine perfection of the Technics SL-1200 model, forever young and forever state-of-the-art in its 1972 design? Perhaps. But whatever it is, maybe we're not ready for our "consumption" of music to wholly resemble what used to be called "data entry." (Kraftwerk *live* was satire, comrades.) Where once you were a kind of magician or midwife or supplicant when you listened to music, laying a needle on top of a spinning and shining circle with utmost care, now what do you do? You catalogue and load and arrange. You used to pan for gold. Now the shit you do to play your music looks exactly like the shit you do to file your taxes. We used to be archeologists rather than technocrats when we went searching for sound. Rentalism represents a new age of the thing versus electronic vapour. (And so on.)

When I read this now, I don't know if I believe it anymore.

A coot, a crank, one of those c words. But the essay explains it simply for the neophyte: It's about touching and being touched. Cradled. How else to put it? You sit in a chair and lift up a magazine, and it's a trip—a track unsuppressed starts to play over a PA. The bass line, let's say. You realize the room is full of objects. Which will release more? You look around, wonder who did this, ask the proprietor, who unaffectedly repeats the slogan, "Nothing's for sale, but you're free to browse." You are it: the stylus, the dial, the tape head, the reel. It's you.

Like after all the snow has melted, and there's a landscape you'd forgotten about; after the rain has sprayed it away, and the sun has come out and you see the colour of grass revealed—that's what this is all about.

Lee, John Pembrey. "Cassette Swan Script." *Bent Borders* 4.1 (June 1984): 21–29. [short fiction]

It's just seven pages long, and the passage that inspired our movement is under a page in length, coming about in the middle of the story. EMG always copied the whole of this scene in longhand and included it somewhere in each of their fronts—framed and hanging above the light switch, silk-screened onto a throw pillow, or scribbled on the bathroom wall.

The story is about an African-American man—"an untethered Negro," he calls himself in the beginning—who wanders up the west coast of North America in the 1970s after losing his job in a soap factory. He listens to an Art Blakey album while dropping some biker-crafted LSD known as Rim Rock Crown Snake, and somehow he interprets the "crown" part of the moniker as a secret message that he must travel to London where, according to his delusion, the Queen will make him immortal. But he has no money for such a flight, of course, and instead hitchhikes up the coast to British Columbia—it being considered by the protagonist a "close second" to Britain itself. All this happens in the first paragraph. The rest of the story takes place in Vancouver, where the protagonist enters a rocky relationship with an unnamed woman, who ultimately leaves him for an Afro-Bavarian ex-boyfriend named Fayrer. The excerpt that is important for our purposes comes at a moment when the protagonist is wandering around Gastown after he's been dumped. Here it is:

> And down the knuckle-colored cobblestones, I happened past that shop, the one that sold nothing, its interior a jumble of unfinished musings and scrambled furniture, this was the one that she said was a song in the form of a store, but free, so here I was, without her, and I went in and up to the desk where a man or a woman, I'm not sure, but someone in a crystal-green waistcoat and blue chemise instructed me to take a number, pointing at the roll on the opposite wall, and I went there and pulled one—zero, as was the next; a whole roll of zip, in fact—and as I ripped the strip of paper from its place the place itself lit up with a walking bass line, stand-up, brandished by, I noticed, two ancient phonograph horns in the north and south corners (petals on a cypress vine), and I sat in a velvet chair and felt the fingers of the unseen

bassist scale around inside my mind, and it was the kind of chair that has a handle at the side that will flip out a built-in foot stool, so I reached down and yanked it up to ease myself back and <<<BAM!>>> the rest of the rhythm section whorled out through the lips of those horns, and I was inside the wiring, in the radio of these people's dreams, Dylan's "green fuse," and the androgyne at the desk looked up and smiled, and so I said, What on Earth?, and this sylph went, Feel free.

I looked around.

I heard there.

I was free to.

Me and Kosei came back to do it all again with a little bit of mescaline three days later, but they'd shut it all up; they'd picked up sticks. Nothing there but a FOR LEASE sign and the reflection of our faces in the storefront's undulating pane...

Rentalists continue to cite Lee and "Cassette Swan Script"; the EMG tradition of including the text of this scene on site is not universal, but is common. I'm not sure what to say about the story beyond its importance to Rentalism. Maybe some of Lee's 1960s-era idealism (and its hallucinatory flip side) may link to the underground and communal impulses of our form. Also, while EMG claim they stumbled upon the story purely by chance, considering Lee's almost total obscurity at that time, one wonders if there's more to it than that, if there's some personal connection. One can let one's mind wander, and imagine other possible layers of depth behind the phenomenon. But that would remain nothing more than speculation.

INTER RIVER PARK

The moment Kurt introduces Allan to his mother, she smiles and keeps it up until after the waiter has come and gone. Her English is better than her son's, and she speaks it with a vaguely British tint. Allan throws around some gilded vocabulary, but it's immediately apparent that it's not going to be enough. He perceives the tension in her face, an inner closure, a barely noticeable withdrawal. Kurt has told him that his mother works in television and Allan wonders if this is her on-screen smile.

Mid-way through the meal, Allan moves to Plan B. He says to Mrs Ma that she has a very fine son, that he knows this for sure because he has noticed that Kurt keeps a picture of her and Mr Ma on his phone, as its "wallpaper." Allan tells Mrs Ma that Kurt obviously keeps it there so that his family is always with him here in Vancouver, so far from home. A very good kid, Allan says. Kurt stays quiet while Allan goes on to tell Mrs Ma that he was inspired by this, and so also put a picture of his mother and father on his phone. I remember when people carried real photographs in their wallets, Allan says wistfully. And he takes his phone out of his pocket, leans forward, and shows it to Mrs Ma across the table. He watches her examine the picture, watches the furrow of uncertainty form on her brow, and then he says what he has rehearsed: That's my mother and my stepfather. My father was a student from Africa—like Barack Obama's father, you know?—but he went back there before I was even born. I never knew him. My mother married later, and they raised me. They are both school teachers.

Mrs Ma looks up at Allan, then back at the picture of the two white strangers that Allan took from the Internet, and he can see that she is working on this, thinking it over. It's like watching someone doing long division in her head. Then she nods faintly.

THOUSANDS OF PEOPLE, mostly students, are on the streets in Québec protesting against tuition increases, banging on pots to show their anger. Allan owes the government $43,000 for his education—for the diction he in turn sells for a living to international students—and he will gladly beat on pots and pans for whomever wants to change the system that resulted in that sum. So he is planning to go to the rally here in Vancouver, in solidarity.

The English language flows through him and out across the surface of the globe. Allan feels it in his very body, an internal sense of complicity.

Who can I borrow a red pot from? From whom can I borrow a red pot?

Allan fixes his language almost as he thinks it.

DEBRIEFING, KURT TELLS Allan that it seems to have worked—that his mother had some words for him about having a tutor who "isn't completely Canadian," as she put it, but she went on to say that Allan seemed studious. Allan waits for more.

And?

Kurt does not look him in the eye, but confesses that his mother also warned him that black people are broken.

Broken?

Broken in the head.

Do you mean "damaged"?

What does "damaged" mean?

Broken.

Yes, I think so. Damaged.

Allan says, Well...

COSTS

- 2 hours concocting false story with Kurt ($60 at $30/hour, tutoring rate)
- Suppressing anger, against being accused of irrational anger
- Several silent prayers, asking my parents' forgiveness

BENEFITS

- 5 hours a week at $30/hour x 6.5 students, against $200/month student loan payment & $600/month shared rent
- Access to Kurt's classmates: Wei is a maybe for 3 hours a week, plus Haoqian and Edith may also be interested
- Kurt is all right, if a little strange, this kid whose real name I don't even know, who laughs loudly but seems shy, who was hung-over once during a session after drinking whisky the night before, who owns a reissued Jag-Stang that he keeps on a guitar stand in the corner of his living room with a sticker on the body that says VANDALISM: BEAUTIFUL AS A ROCK IN A COP'S FACE, who says he has no real friends here, who left behind everything just to get a diploma with the name of a foreign university on it, who stares off into space like he isn't listening but is, who gave me an advanced heads-up about his mom's racism & then stood by me even though he turns mute in her actual presence—he's done more than might be expected. Who am I to him?

FIRE HIM, KURT'S mother says to her son over the phone. She's at the Hotel Georgia. It's 11:15 p.m. Her flight leaves in the morning.

Kurt stammers, Why? I thought you liked him.

The news! I just saw the news on TV and your teacher was on there with a bunch of people shouting and screaming at the police. He was banging on a pot like a madman. He's a hooligan. It's lucky I watched.

Are you sure it was him?

Of course I'm sure!

But maybe it was someone else.

It was him. I can't believe what I have to put up with from you. We wanted you to come here instead of California to keep you away from things like this, and what do you do? You find the only black teacher in this city, somehow.

My grades are good. They've gotten better. He's helped me. I'll ask him about the news. There's probably some mistake.

The only mistake is that we let you live here by yourself! Fire him or we will bring you home. Pei Che is coming next month, and I am going to have to ask him to keep an eye on you if I cannot trust you to act like a normal person.

You don't have to do that.

We will decide what we have to do. Get rid of this crazy person and get a Canadian who doesn't cause trouble in the streets. What kind of teacher does such things? What kind of son treats his mother like this?

KURT MAKES HIS way across the quad. It's the summer intersession so hardly anyone is around. He sees a few students here and there, two workers repairing a door, a groundskeeper. Kurt goes down the stairs, past the library, on toward the bus loop. He walks past the buses, which are lined up against the curb, and heads down the street where the student residences are. He doglegs north, up the incline of the mountain upon which the university is set, and then crosses over to the corner where the equestrian centre is. Kurt walks slowly past the stables, looking at those beautiful animals stuck in their pens. It's a sunny June morning. He's alone. The horses whinny and brap.

Beyond the stable is an enormous park, a collection of half a dozen playing fields for different sports, hewn out of the mountain forest into planes of green. Kurt walks out into the middle of the soccer pitch and lies down. The heat blankets him. He listens to the sound of the world until he drifts away.

ARE YOU ALL right?

Kurt is being shaken. He opens his eyes.

Are you okay?

Two young men are there, one standing above him, the other kneeling at his side, his hand on Kurt's shoulder.

I'm asking if you're okay, mate.

Kurt sits up. Looks around. The three of them are in the field, under the eye of the sun. Then Kurt says something. He speaks to the two men, but the words Kurt says don't mean anything, even as he says them. His mouth is making a sequence of sounds he doesn't recognize.

The two men look at each other. Then the kneeling one says patiently, I'm sorry, buddy, I don't understand. Do you speak English?

Kurt has seen one of them before, in the library, the kneeling one: his turban, his beard, his eyes and mouth always set in such a way that suggests he is ready to smile. The other young man he does not recall seeing before. The two of them are carrying soccer balls, orange cones, a net.

Again Kurt speaks, says something, but it is incomprehensible. He realizes he should, at least, know in his mind what it is he *wants* to say when he speaks, but he does not. He knows his thoughts, when he does not speak, but when he opens his mouth to speak, his mouth and mind are a blur, a slur, a mumble.

The Sikh says, Can you stand? Kurt gets up. Can you understand me? Kurt says something that's nothing. Do you want to walk with us back to the university? Kurt looks around the field and the sky. Though the sun cloaks him with light, he shivers with cold.

The three of them walk toward the campus.

Kurt stops at the stable.

He stands at the fence watching the horses in their stalls.

The two students try to get him to keep going, but Kurt ignores them. When the always-almost-smiling-one gently tugs at his elbow, Kurt doesn't know how to communicate his wishes, so he violently pulls his arm back and screams. The two men back away from Kurt. They look shocked. They talk quietly together. They hover and wonder a while, then finally leave.

Kurt is there alone. He makes no sound.

He is watching a reddish horse, and he is also climbing the fence.

He is standing where he stands, and he is mounting the horse's back.

He is transfixed in his place, and he is letting it take him away, through the gate, up a trail, into the trees.

He is there, and he is riding under layers of leaf-born shadows, cracked by the sun.

He sings a song no one has sung before, and no one anywhere is its audience.

THE BOOM

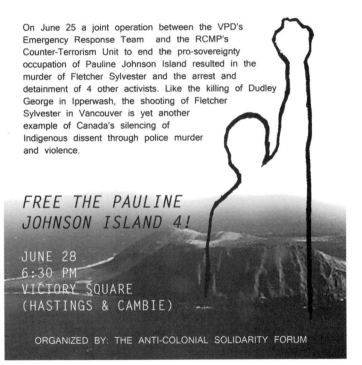

JUSTICE FOR FLETCHER SYLVESTER!

RALLY TO PROTEST THE KILLING OF AN INDIGENOUS POLITICAL ACTIVIST

On June 25 a joint operation between the VPD's Emergency Response Team and the RCMP's Counter-Terrorism Unit to end the pro-sovereignty occupation of Pauline Johnson Island resulted in the murder of Fletcher Sylvester and the arrest and detainment of 4 other activists. Like the killing of Dudley George in Ipperwash, the shooting of Fletcher Sylvester in Vancouver is yet another example of Canada's silencing of Indigenous dissent through police murder and violence.

FREE THE PAULINE JOHNSON ISLAND 4!

JUNE 28
6:30 PM
VICTORY SQUARE
(HASTINGS & CAMBIE)

ORGANIZED BY: THE ANTI-COLONIAL SOLIDARITY FORUM

THE PAULINE JOHNSON ISLAND OCCUPATION: FIVE YEARS AFTER

A RETROSPECTIVE EVENT

Join us as we commemorate the occupation of Pauline Johnson Island and honour the memory of Fletcher Sylvester, killed by the police during the siege five years ago this month. Speakers will include PJI4 members Alison Bartlett and Jean Martin. Music provided by DJ Black Money and Otokoyaku. Spoken word performances by Kempster Fauchet and the Waking Dogs Society. Information on new directions for Indigenous struggle in this region by Klatsassin Adams.

REMEMBER THE FALLEN, CELEBRATE THE RESISTANCE, FIGHT FOR THE FUTURE!

JUNE 12, 7PM
@ THE FLESH & BLOOD CAFE
1657 COMMERCIAL DR.

BY DONATION — PROCEEDS GO TO THE FLETCHER SYLVESTER MEMORIAL FUND

DEMONSTRATION AGAINST THE RE-ZONING OF PAULINE JOHNSON ISLAND

Last year the Canadian government outrageously rescinded Pauline Johnson Island's status as an ecological reserve, green-lighting its official incorporation into the City of Vancouver. We assert that City Hall's recently approved plan to tender a portion of the island for private development should not be allowed to go forward. In the last decade Pauline Johnson Island has become inhabited by a variety of animal and plant life, and is a unique site of global scientific and ecological interest.

VOICE YOUR OPPOSITION TO THIS GRAVE MISUSE OF OUR LAND AND SEA

VANCOUVER CITY HALL
453 W.12TH AVE.
NOV 17
NOON

THE COMMITTEE
FOR AN ECOLOGICALLY
SUSTAINABLE CITY

ARRIVAL is a 10-storey residential tower built on Vancouver's newest waterfront. On Pauline Johnson Island, a "99% safe and dormant volcanic site,"* at the gateway of beautiful Burrard Inlet, ARRIVAL boldly blends the pioneer spirit of Canada's heritage with 21st century bravado.

BE BRAVE. BE THERE. BEGIN.

FLOOR PLAN A
972 SQUARE FT

All suites have a spectacular view of the North Shore, the Strait of Georgia,
the City of Vancouver, and/or the UBC Endowment Lands.

FLOOR PLAN B
1,292 SQUARE FT

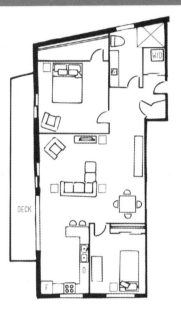

Commercial and retail space on the ground floor of Arrival is
available for lease: www.arrivalresidences/retail.moc

FLOOR PLAN C
862 SQUARE FT

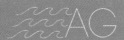

On-call rooftop helicopter service from PJI to Coal Harbour will be available via Air-Burrard.

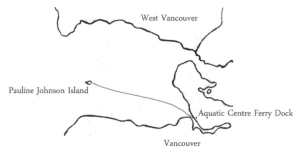

Foot passenger ferry service between PJI and the Aquatic Centre Ferry Dock will include eight sailings per day, and will begin upon completion of the project.

For more information see www.arrivalresidences.moc. Contact us with any questions at arrivalresidences@aniangroup.moc. This is not an offering for sale. For pricing and presentation information, please register by email.

Safety infortmation via a report by the Felix Grant Volcanological Institue. While it is impossible to predict volcanic activity with complete certainty, based on similar conditions worldwide the chance of another significant eruption within thirty years is likely less than one percent. Early detection technology linked to 24/7 evacuation capabilities are included and funded through the strata fee, and eruption insurance options are available. For more information, please see www.arrivalresidences/safety.moc

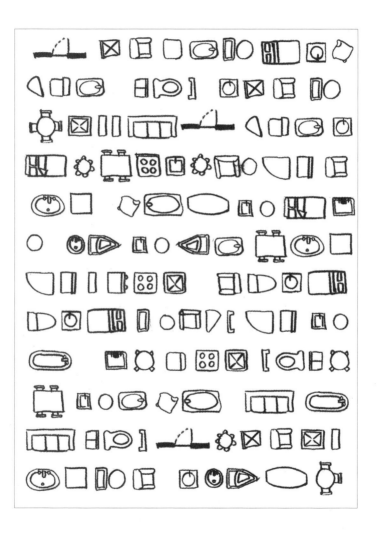

THE SECRET COMMONWEALTH

May pushes her sunglasses up the bridge of her nose with her index finger, her other hand on the wheel of the Sentra. The shades are the only part of her gear that isn't right out of the fourteenth century. She's in a crazy billowing dress with a low neckline, the fabric bunched up beneath her thighs so she can work the pedals unhindered. Her braids are in a topknot, waterfalling down and interwoven with fresh ivy. Everything she's wearing is a variation of green. She, he thinks, is some kind of Afro-dryad.

You're right, Donald says.

She just drives for a while. Then: I'm not the clothing police. I'm just glad we're going together.

Yeah, me too.

Here's the thing, May says. There's a river there, going through the grounds. When you go to bed in your tent, that's the sound you fall asleep to. It really feels like it could be a thousand years ago. You wearing the tunic's not the main thing. The main thing is that feeling.

It's always a thousand years ago, he mumbles.

Feel it, she says.

WHAT IT TURNS out to be, to Donald's eyes, is a field full of people who have hammered themselves into the approximate shapes of a hundred fantasies. No image is left unrealized, from demons to faeries to a man who has somehow pulled off the appearance of a centaur, complete with moving hind-quarters. Some are weirder than the conventional standard of knights and ladies, but the baseline is certainly medieval, with various Eurocentric shadings.

A blond, braided Viking.

A "druid's enclave."

A Middle English language pavilion.

A lecture on tempering your own steel.

And a swordsman incongruously puffing on an asthma inhaler; a Gorgon checking her cell phone. He points out the intrusions of the real world to May, but she just shrugs.

So what? I come here to get away from people telling me I'm wrong about stuff. Not to look for new ways to be wrong about stuff.

The way the Viking looks at May, he notes, is full of unpre-tending desire.

HE JUST CAN'T bring himself to wear what his lover made for him. He can't do it. But, for balance, he stifles the urge to ridi-cule it all through the lens of identity politics.

A black man and woman among… creatures.

The compromise is quietly there, between them, in the field beside the creek.

BARBARIAN-STYLED CATERERS are roasting an actual pig carcass over an open-pit fire. The booze going round is honey mead, mulled wine, and something called "glögg." In addition to the swine, it's all quasi-Dark Ages grub: blood pudding and coarse bread. When they've gotten their food—on wooden instead of paper plates—they sit down on the Persian rug May has brought, which she calls her flying carpet. They eat cross-legged on it, her gown spread out around her like a crushed velvet galaxy. Donald is terrified that the pork is undercooked, having just been twiddled above the fire for who knows how long, but he eats it anyway because he's starving. After the food, the sun dips past the tree line, and the light goes silty. The purchase of fake gold coins is necessary to buy more wine after the first free one, so they get a stack of them and slowly get wrecked on *swiche licour*. Two satyrs get a bonfire going with, impressively, nothing but a rock, a scrap of iron, and a pile of sticks. After a while the only light is from the fire, the moon, and from a few torches carried by those who go back and forth between the campsite and the Port-a-Potties up near the parking lot. Donald can't quite believe they are actually going to sleep here, in this field, with these people. When will the costumes come off?

A sensation goes around the gathering, people talking and craning to see something in one direction at the other side of the fire. There's even some clapping. At first Donald can't see what's going on. Then he spots them: about a dozen figures are at the wood's edge, just visible at the furthest reaches of the firelight. These new arrivals, he can just perceive, are all in black leather, covered with studs; they look like a 1980s heavy metal group without instruments. Their faces are dark, too. Donald strains to comprehend what he's looking at, then he realizes they've smudged their faces with dark makeup. They're white people who've blackened up, like minstrels.

Shadow Realmers, May says matter-of-factly. Well, technically they are Spectres, who are like a sub-species of the Shadow Realmers. They live underground during the day and only come to the surface at night.

What are you talking about?

May waves her hand in front of her face, as if to clear away smoke—the smoke of his ignorance, he thinks.

They've jumbled together a bunch of different myths, she says. There's a whole story behind it. It would take a long time to explain.

They look like Al Jolson playing *Mad Max*.

Cosplay, she says. Go with it.

What do you mean, they live underground?

They live in a vast network of underground caverns beneath the realm, hundreds of layers deep. Are you okay?

A thought flares through Donald like a nova. A fear of heights—no, of *depth*; he once saw a documentary about this; a couple, one who was a hoarder and one who was afraid of long hallways, bridges, gulfs of void, and empty space. A character like this takes shape in Donald's brain. The character, with this fear, meets these subterranean fantasists. Their imaginary depth is his habituation therapy. He sketches out the whole story in his mind, in an instant. Just a sketch. But there it is, the core.

He tells it to her. And asks: Can you introduce me to them? May hesitates. Sure. Yeah. Fiction? About them?

No, he says. Fiction about the fictional character I'm thinking of. Not about them. Or me. Or you. But yeah, fiction. I don't know for sure, yet.

Donald's gut vibrates with excitement. He feels as if he is evaporating. He feels as if his heart is changing. It becomes unclosed, but hard, like a bucket or a bowl. A container full of smaller, softer hearts, Donald decides.

DONALD JUST HAPPENED to be in his girlfriend's neighbourhood that particular afternoon. He'd met with a friend at a café a few blocks from Cassandra's place, so he decided to drop in on her unannounced, to see if she was home. But only May, her roommate, was there. Cassandra, she said, was on call and had to go in to work. Donald hesitated, and May invited him in.

She had a little weed, and they got the TV going, a show about earthquakes. One of them suggested they do a simulation of the procedures spelled out on the show. (The Big One will hit Vancouver one day; it's just a matter of time—no joke.) They got under the coffee table, but decided it was too small and fragile. They finally decided the front hall was the safest, but had to remove the metal toolbox from the top shelf of the closet—those doors would fly open, the box would cave their heads in. They got back on the couch, watched the show some more. Donald excused himself to the bathroom, but instead surprised her by lifting the sofa, hoisting one corner, and May shrieked with laughter, saying, That's not shaking, that's just tipping! So he dropped it and dove at her, lifting her feet in the air as if he was going to pick her up and shake her, and she howled with laughter and shouted, Okay! Okay! Okay! But Donald said, There's no escape! He zoomed down, waving his hands around as if to tickle her, and May was deflecting them, laughing and crying. And suddenly Cassandra was there in the doorway staring at them. Donald got up and said, What? May sat up and said, Earthquake? She straightened her clothes. Cassandra stood there. Donald took one step toward her, and Cassandra, as if in answer, gently set her arm down on the sideboard next to the door like she was going to lean on it. But instead she swept everything off the surface, sending all of it to the floor—the framed photographs, the books, two of May's dragon's head candlesticks. Her arm glided across the top like a well-fitted windshield wiper, and that was how that particular afternoon went.

MAY INTRODUCES DONALD to a Spectre who is clutching a black mug with the embossed image of a spider on it. In addition to the makeup, he has black polish on his fingernails. A medieval Lou Reed. The man says, You should join us. We've been trying to acquire Lady May here for ages. But she won't be corrupted.

I'd love for you to take me to the caverns, Donald says.

The Spectre just looks at him. What do you mean?

May told me you live underground. You've got a network of caves or whatever. I'd like to see them. Donald fishes in his pockets for the bag of fake gold coins, the ones they bought their weird booze with. He thrusts it at the guy.

The Spectre looks at May, his eyes seeking her help. May bumps the look back over to Donald.

Look, Donald says, I know there aren't really caverns. But I don't care. I want you to take me down there. Do you understand?

There's a moment. The Spectre squints. Then nods vigorously. Ah, says the guy, as if everything suddenly makes sense. Okay, right. You want to be *initiated.*

Donald shakes his head, waves the idea off. I just wanna *go* there.

The Spectre looks puzzled, but tugs at his earlobe, like he's really thinking about it. Well, he says, I could talk to our Head Revenant.

Yeah, talk to whoever. Just take me there, show me around. Twenty minutes, that's all. You keep those coins.

When the Spectre leaves, May asks him, What are you doing?

Going native, he says.

DON'T LEAVE ME, she whispers.

I won't, he tells her automatically.

They are in their tent by the side of the river.

Really, she says. I mean it.

Mean what? He's thinking about the worlds.

They lay holding each other for a long time. The sound of moving water. He can feel the alcohol in him ebbing away. Before he knows it, her breathing is regular and deep, and she's snoring gently.

Donald remembers what it is like to be afraid. To be anxious. Imagines an anxiety attack. He closes his eyes, recalls the times in his life when his innards turned to slush and his fingertips went bloodless with stress. Car accidents.

Arguments. Breakups. Donald yawns, and settles into his own mind.

HE WAKES UP.

He sees light through the skin of the tent. Fire? Torches. Shadows.

Come out, says a voice from the other side. The voice is female. It says, We are here for the one they call Donald.

May stirs beside him. She says, What's going on?

The woman out there says, You are summoned. If you agree to walk with us, come out and be initiated!

Donald smiles in the tent, in the dark. He sits up, parts the flap. Can she come too? He says it through the door to the half dozen dark ones standing out there in the torchlight.

There is a pause. Some low voices. Then: No. It will be you and you alone.

He backs off, closes the flap, starts to put on his clothes. He dons the tunic.

Don't go, May says. Her voice is shaking. He can hear her breathing rapidly.

Don't worry, Donald says, I'll be back in twenty minutes. How long can this take? Half an hour, I bet.

No, really, I don't want you to go.

He kneels beside her. Why? He looks at her in the dim light that filters through the sides of the tent. Seriously, I'll be back in a flash. These are your friends, anyway, right?

She's quiet, but he can feel her rigidity. He reaches for her face, cups her cheek, leans to kiss her. Her lips are hard.

Donald leaves the tent and stands among them. She's back

in there alone. He wonders if she's safe—all these costumed nuts around—and says to the Head Revenant, I don't want to leave her here all by herself. But the woman, her face as black as the sky, says, We'll keep watch. She'll be fine. It's *you* you should be concerned about.

Two of the shadows gently put their hands on his shoulders, guiding him into a space between the trees, a trailhead he hadn't discerned during the day. They walk beside and just behind him, as if Donald's been arrested. He thinks of purges, recruitments, conscriptions. He's a guerrilla, an enemy combatant. He isn't going to the unassailable high ground. This is descent.

He says to the phantasm at his elbow, What's going to happen?

The shadow-man seems to think about this for a while. Then he says, It is like taking a sword and melting the steel. Then re-casting it into a better sword. You will be re-created, re-forged. You will not, the shadow says, be who you once were. Nothing will ever be the same.

And with that they make him real.

WHEN DONALD GETS back to their campsite, the tent is gone. There's no sign of May. His backpack, the only thing left, is sitting on the ground. He looks at one of the Spectres, who was supposed to be keeping watch on her. Where is she?

He breaks character: She totally left, bro.

Donald looks around. It's after midnight in a forest three municipalities from the city. All that's in his bag is a change of clothes, his toothbrush, comb.

He makes his way up to the parking lot, tripping on rocks and roots, on the dark uneven ground. When he finally gets to where the Sentra was parked, it's not there. He stands where it was and looks up at the stars, puts his hands on his head.

Nice shirt.

It's the voice of a woman, two parking spaces to his left, in a van. Its side door is open and she's in the back there with maybe two others. They're lighting something and passing it around—a joint or a pipe. The lone light on the other side of the lot doesn't quite reach the inside of the van.

Tunic, Donald says. Did you see a woman leave here in a black sports car?

The owner of the voice says, Yup, I saw her.

He approaches them. The woman who spoke sparks a lighter, applies it to what he can now see is definitely a pipe. The bowl of it is a glass *nazar*—an eye of warding—and when she's done, she passes it to one of the other women.

She left?

About an hour ago.

Donald digs in his pocket for his phone, but before he gets it out, she informs him that it won't work.

This is the back of beyond, she says.

I can't stay here, he says. I gotta get home.

They ignore him while they futz with the dope, finally passing it around again. One of them turns on the interior light. It's now that he notices that all three have silver hair. They're young women, but they seem made-up to look aged. When it's finally the first one's turn once more, the loamy smoke spews forth. She points the stem of the pipe out at the darkness. There's a late bus that goes into town. The closest stop is down at the turn-off, she says.

Could I walk there?

She checks the time on the dash. Not if you want to make the bus, no.

One of her friends says, Forget it. We can't drive him. I'm crashing in ten.

Sorry, says the first one. Guess we can't help you.

He takes out his wallet. Twenty bucks. Just drop me off at the stop. If I miss it, I'll try to hitch from the highway.

The third woman, who hasn't spoken yet, leans over and whispers something in the first woman's ear. Then the first one speaks up again: How about this. We'll give you a lift if you sign over to us.

Sign over?

You registered when you got here, right? Did you keep your game receipt?

Donald fishes for it in his pocket. He shows them.

Pass it here. The third woman reaches out and he gives it to her. She fires the lighter and for a second he thinks she's going to torch it, but she's just reading. Yeah, she says. He's paid up for a whole cycle. She hands it back to him.

The first woman nods, like she's thinking. Then she goes through her purse. Okay, she says, handing him a pen. Write down "To the Republic of the Graeae" on the back and sign your name below it. And put your password at the bottom. We'll take it to the Magister in the morning and divvy up your essence points. You're out anyway, right?

I'm out. He signs.

Hop in.

DONALD LOOKS THROUGH the half-mirror of the bus window at the landscape. It reels by. The country will become the suburbs, and the suburbs will become the city, and then he'll be home. The exterior is dark. Subterranean walls of black.

What they'd wanted was for him to turn May, to get her to join their group. It was transparent from the start, though they couched everything in the patois of their game. If he could convince May to come over to their crew, they would take him too, and let him in on all their arcane rules and protocols. But it wasn't even really May they wanted. She had, according to them, a sacred object, the Jewel of Something-or-Other—a token of gameplay. It took them half an hour of jabbering there in the torch-lit clearing to get to that point. The Jewel would give them the power to counter the Kingdom of Somebody-or-Other. He stopped paying attention and interrupted. Asked to leave. The magic of the moment was broken and his interest in the concept melted into the night air.

And here he is alone in the howl of the bus on the highway.

The driver has shut off the interior lights. It's just Donald in the back and the driver up front, no one else. He tries to get comfortable for the long ride, hugs his bag, and rests his head against his own reflection in the window. A cold echo. He closes his eyes and waits for the change.

400 FT³ (11.33 M³)

━━ ━━ ━━ ━━

Troy slides the desk into the space beneath the window, wondering how he will get any work done with such a view in front of him: the North Shore mountains, the bridge, the park, the city. The water looks like the surface of a vast jewel. Only a ship here and there mars the image. He thinks about all the times he has gazed out at the harbour from the city. Now he is there, as if by magic, but really by credit and daring.

There are boxes everywhere yet to be unpacked. But Troy wants the desk and computer available. They will pin him down here, make this space his. Jatinder is doing something similar in the living room, deep in the trance of arranging and re-arranging.

When he gets down on his hands and knees to plug in a cord, he sees a corner of paper sticking out from the back of the drawer.

The desk is new to him, though he grew up with it all his life. It was his father's first, then his mother's. Now it's his. Troy remembers watching his father carefully doing his taxes at the desk when he was a child, and he remembers seeing all the things left untouched on the desktop for years, it seemed, after his father had gotten sick. His mother did not begin to use the desk herself until Troy moved out of the house and went to university in another city. The desk is scored and old. Dark heavy wood.

The surface is a field of mourning. But the underside seems cheap.

A corner of paper pointing down.

He can't work it free without ripping it, so he removes the drawer, and there it is, an envelope stapled to the back, crumpled, askew. He tears it away. It's yellow and old. Inside is a single folded sheet of paper. Cursive in blue—

Delman Kern (1833–1897) [3/4 black, 1/4 white] m.
   (mulatto woman)

begat
John Kern Sr (1867–1932) [5/8 black, 3/8 white] m.
   (Nootka woman)

begat
John Kern Jr (1889–1958) [5/16 black, 3/16 white, 1/2 Indian]
   m. (quadroon woman)

begat
William Kern (1923–1981) [9/32 black, 15/32 white, 1/4
   Indian] m. (white woman)

begat
Daniel Kern (1952–) [9/64 black, 47/64 white, 1/8 Indian] m.
   (white woman)

begat
Troy Kern (1983–) [9/128 black, 111/128 white, 1/16 Indian]

His father's handwriting.
　He reads it.
　He reads it.
　He reads it very slowly.
　Jatinder enters the room, steps over the boxes to get to him.
He hands the piece of paper to her.
　After a time she says, Did you—?
　No.
　So this is—?
　New to me. Yeah.
　Her brow is furrowed. What does this mean?
　I don't know.
　She flips the paper over. Scans it. Then hands it to him.
　On the other side it says, HISTIAIOS. STEGANOGRAPHY.
HOW?

HE SEARCHES THROUGH three boxes before he finds it: *A Boy's Book of Codes*, by Anthony Saxelford (London: Ark Press, 1960). The memory is in his fingertips. He flips to it automatically:

> Histiaios believed his only chance to escape Susa was for Aristagoras to start the rebellion in Miletos, which would draw attention away from his position. But the roads between Susa and Miletos were heavily patrolled by the enemy. Any messenger he sent would be searched. So Histiaios summoned his most trusted slave, shaved

the hair from his head, and instructed his scribe to tattoo the plans for revolt on the slave's scalp using a needle and ink. He waited until the slave's hair grew in and then sent him on to Miletos. When the slave arrived he asked that Aristagoras shave his head, revealing Histiaios's orders to rebel. In this way Histiaios ensured that his meticulous instructions would be received in his own wording, as he distrusted the commitment of such a critical message to the memory and care of a subordinate.

There's an asterisk scribbled by his father in the margin beside the passage.

When his dad gave him this book, Troy was seven years old. By then his father had been sick for a year and a half, and would die seven months and eight days later.

He flips to the title page and there it says: TO TROY, FROM DAD, FOR EVER.

HIS BACK IS to the large mirror, the one in the freestanding frame. It was his mother's, had always been hers. She stood in front of it every day; it was as tall as she was, made of magenta pine, she said.

(No such thing.)

Whatever she knew, she took it with her, too.

He angles the handheld mirror over his shoulder, aiming it here and there at the back of his head.

Nothing.

There is a mess of his hair on the floor.

Jatinder watches him from the edge of the bed.

He steps backwards, toward himself, closer. He throws his head back to expose his crown, bends the tops of his ears over with his fingers, swivels this way and that.

Nothing. Nowhere.

Okay. What now?

Troy lets his hand—the one holding the smaller mirror—drop to his side.

This is crazy.

Jatinder nods.

He kneels beside her. He closes his eyes and rests his face against her thigh. His head feels too cool, as if it were wet.

She touches his scalp. She's never seen him bald before. Her fingers move lightly across his skin.

What did they call that ridiculous thing they used to do, diagnosing people by feeling the bumps on their heads?

They called it "science."

THE NAME OF the place is TERMINAL SELF STORAGE. It sounds to Troy like a joke or a judgment.

He opens the latch on the old trunk.

Toys he's kept. Action figures, an old green army tank, countless interlocking plastic bricks. Tears. Immediately. The smell of these things, a mix of polymer, dust, cardboard. The sudden currents of memory—Christmas, birthdays. Then a black garbage bag, beneath it all, taped up. He rips it open. The musty plush animals, the familiar colours and shapes. The texture of his making. The scents of his house and the everyday of his childhood somehow stowed here, which is nowhere.

And finally the one he is after. The one he called Harold Brown.

Because his father had called it that.

Troy tries to remember its origins. A birthday maybe.

But the reason he is here is because of his father's refrain, only now glaring out in relief, that he should never throw the doll away, even when he was grown. That he should pass it on to his own son someday.

A woolly explosion of black hair. Harold Brown's button eyes, his faded and tattered grey suit made of terrycloth.

Troy lifts him up to the fluorescent light hanging from the corrugated ceiling of the ten-by-five locker. Parts the hair at the back of the doll's head. The yarn is frayed and matted. No other way. He takes the scissors out of his jacket pocket and cuts a path.

There on the scalp, stitched inexpertly, needle and thread in red on the doll's cloth skin: a site, a street, a set of numbers, an inexorable accounting.

The button-eyes look.

That endless stare.

WHY IS IT just boys? Sons?

I don't know. "Primogeniture"—is that the word?

"Patriarchy" is what you're looking for.

THEY TAKE THE ferry from the island to the Aquatic Centre Dock, then walk over to the lot where they keep their car. It doesn't take long to drive to the East Hastings address, which was the whole of the message stitched onto the doll's scalp. When they get there, parking across from it, the whole block is the skeleton of a building. A crane sprouts out of it. Workers, cement trucks, rebar.

They watch the revision of the city through the glass.

The address is the same, but that Vancouver is gone.

2BR + SPECTACULAR VIEW

According to the directories they pick through at the library, the space had been home to many things over the years—all industrial usages, though it has now been rezoned: an auto parts shop; a pressure washer rental store; a seller of trolley wheels and castors. But in the last years of Troy's father's life the address is listed as "Lennox and Sons, book publishers." The proprietor is down as "A. Lennox."

ALL MOD CONS

A variety of searches. The footprints of the last century. And finally a used book, a slim thing, at a store in Oberlin, Ohio, via the computer. He puts it in his "cart":

The Elucidation Proclamation: 100th Anniversary Edition
George S. Lennox (author)
Paperback: 108 pages
Publisher: Spectrum Continental Communications
    (Vancouver, BC, 1958)
Language: English

Product Dimensions: 5.5 x 0.7 x 8 inches

Average Customer Review: <u>Be the first to review this item</u>

OPEN CONCEPT

"We are as a prism reversed: our hues go into the glass and come out colorless and, like light, we retain the potential of our former state. We look back, and we act with fidelity. Our achievements will never be measured. We will never be comprehended as heroes. The Race will never celebrate our victories in story or song. Our offensives will be as subtle as pen strokes and our conquests as bland as handshakes. In plain sight we will fight a war that no one, not even the Enemy, will understand is being waged. And when we win, our Race will not know how or why they won; they will only know that they are victors. Our Enemy will not know that he has been defeated, but he will be outflanked. We will make an ever expanding net, a snare, of what are now clear battle lines. We will change the unchangeable from within.

"Such are the principles of this, our long strategy to overwhelm the forces of complexional distinction that have cast a shadow on this continent since our arrival in chains. We hereby call these principles to which we adhere 'Hannibalism' after the great African who in similar style entered the Enemy's house to defeat him from the inside. His were the Alps into Italy; ours are the sly routes of blood and reflection. We will win where his work was unfinished.

"Yet Hannibal is merely one source of inspiration. The other is the figure of our current political governor, a man whom rumor without confirmation asserts has colored ancestry, though his looks are as those of a white man. With this secret tucked away in the feint of his visage, he rose to the highest rank in the region, and now cannot be touched by word from British Guyana and elsewhere that his mother was a plantation Mulatto, his father a Scottish exploiter. James Douglas, a builder of this fort and of these colonies, is the unsteady hand behind our immigration to these shores from those United States. But he is no friend to the Long Project, and his motives are personal only. Nevertheless, in his eyes and countenance I found the suggestion of a way out of this wilderness for us. One Douglas can do nothing. But a secret army of them could change all.

"Hannibalism is, simply put, the deliberate tactic of marrying light and creating issue who are lighter skinned than oneself and passing this practice on to one's eldest. This itself does nothing but make a singular kind of escape and is in form nothing new. But we add the crucial formula, an intergenerational strategy, to also pass on with this tradition the Secret Mission to use this skin, this guise, this lightened body, to enter the house of Oppression and loosen its hinges. As our descendants lighten, so will their status and power increase, and with the Secret Mission passed on, they will be whites in body but Negroes in mind, spirit, and action. Judges, doctors, politicians, lawyers, makers of doctrine and policy will emerge forth as white men to the outward world but men whose power will be used to elevate the status of our Race at each turn, and end our oppression. This is the future cabal that we will build.

"Above all, the Mission must remain clothed in silence. These documents may be circulated freely, but your own allegiance to its principles must remain internal. Passing on the

Mission to your sons must be done when they are just coming of age, and they must be carefully brought into this as into the most exclusively guarded guild. All must be kept from those closest to you. The line goes forward for ever. The silent victory is at hand. As it says in Second Corinthians: 'We look not at the things which are seen, but at the things which are not seen: for the things which are seen are temporal; but the things which are not seen are eternal.' We go into the future bearing the Race in our hearts always."

JATINDER IS REALLY the handy one, but he has a go at putting the crib together. The instructions are in twelve languages, with dowels and a hex key. When he's done, there are pieces left over. But it is as sturdy as anything.

Troy has heard that there is a growing clear-cut the size of a small country in the middle of Siberia, where the manufacturer of the crib gets all its wood. The world, now the world of his coming child, a future world, is an island of growing but unseen debts and consequences. A mass of plastic flotsam in the Pacific. A patch of apocalyptic void in a foreign forest.

Who assembled the pieces of this that he assembles in turn?

He will pass on every single thing.

And the years will come and go with the tides, taking what they take and leaving what they leave.

The blocks are interlocking, and with them his girl will build a little house on the floor of her bedroom. For her "babies."

He will watch, transported by pure awe.

FINAL REPORT

━ ━ ━ ━

ASSOCIATION FOR PETROSOMATOGLYPHIC INNOVATION

Clandestine Placement Grant

Funding is available through our Clandestine Placement program for the following categories of self-directed projects involving impressions of hands, feet, faces, or other body parts into rock, concrete, brick, or other like materials. Our two funding channels include:

Site-specific: Creating and installing permanent, unaccredited, socially engaging petrosomatoglyphs, in urban or rural settings, for the purpose of inspiring new ways of thinking about familiar sites and/or for referring in innovative ways to pre-existing historical or cultural understandings of these sites.

Peripatetic: Creating mobile, unaccredited, socially engaging petrosomatoglyphs, imprinted in a subject material that can be placed in a public space and subsequently found, moved, stolen, sold, stored, recovered, and otherwise passed from hand-to-hand by the general public. (These must be impressed into materials weighing no more than twenty kilograms.)

The maximum amount of funding available per application is $5,000.

Eligible Recipients: Canadian citizens; Canadian non-profit organizations; Canadian municipalities and townships.

Applicants must include a design sketch, a one-page project description, and a CV.

Due date: January 31

THE LOGATOMIC INSTITUTE

The Angus Nanning Bursary for Studies in Comparative Non-Lexical Vocalism

The Logatomic Institute is pleased to offer this bursary for the purposes of offsetting the burden of tuition. Members of the Alumni Association have dedicated this to the late Angus Nanning for his contributions to the field of comparative non-lexical vocalism.

We are currently accepting applications from students who wish to receive this bursary and who are working on a project involving the translation of a significant extant sample of lilting, mouth music, scat singing, and/or other forms of non-lexical vocalism into a similarly non-lexical form including, but not specific to, lilting, mouth music, scat singing, and/or other forms of non-lexical vocalism.

The bursary amount is $5,750. It will go to a single recipient.

Applicants must answer the question below and send it to *klactoveedsedstene@tli.moc*. Please paste your answer into the body of your email; do not send attachments. Please also include your name, age, address, and phone number.

Question:

Without using words or images, explain why you think you should receive this bursary and how it would improve your ability to research the forms you are investigating.

(Note: We also require two wordless/imageless letters of recommendation indicating why you are a worthy candidate for this bursary. It is not important that these arrive with your application, but it is required that they are drafted, and we recommend that applicants leave each letter in a location near, but not necessarily at, the Institute, such as unfolded upon a rock at Pigeon Bluff, near the stone plinth that overlooks Armleder's farm, where the wind may or may not lift and carry it until it rests at a place where it may or may not be read by someone who may or may not influence, in conversation or through action, the life of one [or more] of the jury members, toward a positive or negative outcome in the selection process involving you or some other future candidate.)

The closing date for applications is March 22.

THE SOCIETY FOR CREATIVE INTOXICATION

The Society for Creative Intoxication is currently accepting applications for the funding and development of performance-based work that depicts the influence of original fictitious psychoactive drugs in public settings. This year the SCI celebrates its twenty-fifth year as an organization, and has created the following grant in order to enrich the practice of creative and/or narrative intoxication.

WHO IS ELIGIBLE

Anyone who is nineteen years or older—and who can perform in the Greater Vancouver Regional District on any date within one calendar year of being selected—is eligible for this award.

HOW TO APPLY

Provide a written description of your originally created fictitious stimulant, narcotic, or hallucinogen. This description must be no more than 500 words in length. Be sure to include your name and preferred contact method in the spaces provided. Mail to the address below. Handwritten descriptions are preferred. Applications must be received no later than November 17.

ADJUDICATION

A committee composed of senior SCI members (in good standing) will create a shortlist of the best three applications.

The top three applicants will then be contacted and asked to audition at the SCI office, providing an early "sketch" of their performance. (For out-of-town applicants, a video audition is acceptable.) From this shortlist, the committee will then award a grant winner, a runner-up, and an honorable mention. The latter two will not receive funding but will be cited in all communications and press releases.

PAYMENT AND PERFORMANCE

The winning applicant will be awarded $10,000 and will be expected to complete their performance within one year of receiving the grant. Performances may last any period of time (depending on the side-effects of your fictional drug), and must take place in any public setting within Metro Vancouver. Traditionally, performances are not announced, but are rather received by the public without knowing they are witnessing a performance. Actors are asked to refrain from excessively aggressive or offensive work, and are responsible for keeping their performance within the limits of the law. The SCI is not responsible for performances that transgress public order.

OUR ADDRESS

Submit all correspondence to:

Performance Grant Selection Committee
The Society for Creative Intoxication
738 E. Ginger Goodwin Blvd.
Vancouver, BC V6A 2ΩA

THE NORTH AMERICAN COUNCIL OF
PSYCHOGEOGRAPHICAL BROADCASTERS

The North American Council of Psychogeographical Broadcasters' philanthropic grant stream for independent radio networks operating in the medium of In Situ Counterfactual Traffic Reporting is open to ongoing applications.

Our In Situ Counterfactual Traffic Reporting grants assist the creation and maintenance of temporary and mobile radio stations, in any metropolitan area in Canada or the United States, for the purpose of broadcasting imaginary traffic reports for imaginary cities during high volume commuting periods in actual cities, receivable by car radios within a radius of one kilometre (0.6 miles) or more.

Applications eligible for funding may make reference to alternate and imagined streets, freeways, bridges, tunnels, public transit, ferry routes, and other systems. Counterfactual traffic reporting may blend your locale's actual infrastructural points of reference with imagined cityscapes (for heightened disorientation) or may be wholly mythical. Similarly, "traffic" can be freely interpreted and need not refer to conventional vehicles but may include anachronistic or speculative transportation technologies, beasts of burden, mutated locomotive abilities, teleportation, subterranean burrowing, propulsion by extrasensory perception, weather control, ludic determination, and so on.

Deadlines: January 11, May 11, September 11.

Maximum Support: $50,000.

Recommended Submission Elements:

1. A textual treatment of your broadcast.

2. A detailed map of your imagined cityscape (if applicable).

3. A project budget.

4. A production timeline.

5. Reference to your experience with extralegal broadcasting and knowledge thereof.

(Interested parties may apply without use of real names, or as groups using pseudonymous call-signs.)

After breaking the code below, submit your application to the address revealed. Please provide your return address and/or email address in a comparably difficult code.

X#A(((XD #)))#DY+
^HMMM, LI$%)))(((#
GK!!!*H
_.::_

SUBJECTIVE JOY FOUNDATION

Who looks outside, dreams. Who looks inside, awakens.
—Carl Jung

Nominations are currently being accepted for individual candidates to our Simulation of Bliss (Long Term) program unit. Groups interested in nominating a candidate are to submit an application with the following specifications:

Eligible candidates must ...

... be practicing artists or political activists, with a reasonable expectation that these activities will be part of their lifelong development.

... be of reasonable physical health (to ensure a substantial tenure).

... be citizens of Canada.

... have no connections to the Foundation, professionally or socially.

Nominating applicants must be composed of groups of seven or more people. For notes on group structure and annual reporting requirements, see NOTES ON GROUP STRUCTURE AND ANNUAL REPORTING REQUIREMENTS.

In accordance with Our Founder's belief that self-actualized joy is largely, if not entirely, a matter of subjective experience, and that the mind-events of one are the mind-events of all, our Simulation of Bliss (Long Term) remuneration program is available as an award to a group of applicants committed to, ideally, the decades-long (or, perfectly, life-long) project of singling out one deserving artist or activist and targeting him or her with the tactic of Expansive Ensconcing—whereby the artist or activist is, without his or her knowledge, buoyed up "behind the curtain" by our committee—i.e., shadowed, supported, and made, as much as our team can achieve, successful, on their terms, which become, by proxy enjoyment, our terms also. Selected applicants will buy the artist's art, bestow funds upon him or her through front-group grants, publish positive reviews, blogs, books, theses, and dissertations praising the target; winning applicants will follow their activist or artist through his or her various endeavours, which they will support from the penumbra of the target's life, leaving the development and theory to him or her, honouring this reservoir of bliss. In the form of supposed citizens' groups, you will heap upon them letters of support and written profiles, stage demonstrations and incidents that coat the target in the lustre of heroism, advance the candidate's particular ideological or artistic bent in as much subtle and specific detail as you can summon, without thought to your own beliefs. In this way you will make this one subject's singular genius or revolutionary role real, and you, from without, will harvest the ecstasy you have sown—proximately, quietly, vicariously, voraciously.

Endowment Release

$7 million (CAD)

For the current application form, see CURRENT
APPLICATION FORM.

SOCIAL ECONOMICS FORUM

Crisis, Crash, and Chronometry Grant

The prestigious C3 Grant from the Social Economics Forum (the research wing of the Undollaring Society) is administered with the intention of funding projects that develop original time-keeping and calendrical systems drawn from the cycles of market collapse.

Past recipients include—

—Julia Besse, for a bubble clock that expands in volume relative to the value of the Dow Jones Industrial Average multiplied by years since the last crash

—George Goçgulyýew, for a Stonehenge-inspired megalithic astronomical calendar set to twentieth- and twenty-first-century recessions and recoveries

—Alex Brady, for a digital, Wi-Fi-capable pocket watch with a webcrawling bot that paces the gears to tick only when it finds the phrase "economic crisis" in the headline of a news site

Apply by sending a detailed description of your project to:

Box 17
983 Arrow St.
Vancouver, BC
V6A 9O9

Your application must be received by January 15. The grant value is $5,000 CAD.

COMMITTEE FOR THE INSTATEMENT OF PARACOSMIC ARTS COMMITTEES

Many people mentally build towns, cities, countries, and empires as a form of serialized daydreaming. The creation of paracosms is more common among children than adults. Some, however, like the Brontë sisters or C.S. Lewis, continue to dream of these imagined realms of their childhood well into adult life.

We at the Committee for the Instatement of Paracosmic Arts Committees (CIPAC) have initiated a new program for those with active paracosms who are interested in adding a cultural mandate to the world they have created through their own private Genesis. That is, if you are interested in your inner world having a healthy local, national, or international arts infrastructure, including material support as well as support in the form of official honours, then our program may be for you.

While we anticipate the definition of "art" in your paracosm may include visual art, music, theatre, dance, writing, film, digital media, and so on—that is, the broadest definition of creative practices—we also understand that specific paracosms may have unique and unusual traditions and forms. CIPAC embraces such diversity and we encourage our jurors to consider this when examining forms that operate beyond the bounds of standard, real-world genres.

Our funding is for, but is not limited to, the following types of in-paracosm development:

- Establishing an institutional body with the funding and expertise to disburse grants aimed at whatever arts are important in your paracosm's cultural milieu.

- Building a system of arts awards and prizes, public, private, or mixed in funding origins, for new and established artists.

- The establishment of artist residencies, festivals, conferences, centres, schools, galleries, and archives.

- The creation of advanced social support for artists such as pensions, retirement homes for artists, the use of artists in public health initiatives, education, trauma recovery, conflict resolution, rehabilitation of violent offenders, and other projects considering art in the social sphere.

TO APPLY

Please create a detailed description of your paracosm, with particular focus on its artistic and cultural life.

Your description should be no more than twenty pages, and should include some indication of the government or social organization most amenable to housing our proposed committee.

Your application should not be sent. Once completed, it will be sent for; it will be sensed and will attract those within our fictions who circulate, seek, and locate such desires. These agents will smell the yearning your application exudes. They will arrive at the site of your application. They will see through the aperture of your application. They will self-form in your space and appear or filter through or settle there, with you, like moss on a yew or damp on a dockside bollard. These agents will appear according to your abilities of perception— shapes of heavy smoke, ash-light swarms, swallowed laughs with eyes—these will come to collect your proposal.

Approved applications will be appointed a CIPAC officer who will initiate the process of organizing an active and vibrant arts infrastructure in your paracosm within thirty days.

You will know in your heart if your application has been successful.

You'll feel it beginning.

THE OUTER HARBOUR

━━ ━━ ━━ ━━

The girl is standing on the rooftop, staring at herself.

Her corpse is on the gurney. She knows that the body is lifeless, but they do not, so the people from the city are trying to save her. She stands beside them as they work, looking down into her own hollow eyes.

They wheel the bed to the helicopter and load it in. The chatter of the blades shatters the moment.

Her parents are not allowed to go with her body and are forced to watch the helicopter rise into the black sky and veer toward the lights on the shore across the water. She watches her parents watching them take her away.

On the roof of the ten-storey building, standing on a massive white "H" enclosed by a circle, left behind are five staff members, the girl, and her mother and father.

Eventually the staff escort her parents back to their unit. She follows. Watches them weep and scream in their home.

When she can't take any more, she learns how to leave.

Review of *Mercenary Dreaming: A Curious Story of How
  Fantasy Gaming Innovated the Technology of Repression*
  (89 mins., Documentary, Dir: Donald Abbey)

The most important adjective in the title of this new documentary, which premiered at the Vancouver International Film Festival this week, is definitely the word "curious"—because, like the line spoken by Alice upon entering Wonderland, the tale that first-time filmmaker Donald Abbey gives us gets curiouser and curiouser as it goes. If your interest is piqued by the unlikely connection between play and policing, then the free-fall down this particular rabbit hole will prove well worth the vertigo.

How curious? Well, the film begins with the director's own strange personal journey as a conjoined twin who grew up in Vancouver and survived an operation severing him from his brother. Before being separated, the twins had a brief musical career together. That seems like quite enough to be the entire topic of a film, but that's not at all what this documentary is about. In fact, Abbey's background is summarized in a voiced-over montage before the real story begins, tangentially enough, when the director becomes involved with a Vancouver-based LARP—a "live action role-playing" game that is like a cross between a Renaissance fair and puzzle-solving collective theatre. In the documentary, Abbey describes how he became obsessed with the game—which is called "The Secret Commonwealth"—after being introduced to it by his ex-girlfriend, and how his initial intention was to make a feature film about a character who is similarly drawn in. But in the process of filming, something else emerges—namely, the shadowy figure of the game's creator, Jamie Langenderbach, who leads the strange subculture of fans involved in the Secret Commonwealth. (The name comes from the title of a centuries-old Scottish guidebook about mythical creatures.) What begins as a film about making a film soon becomes a real-life mystery, as Abbey tries to get a fix on the man behind the curtain.

The key detail that initially puts Langenderbach on the filmmaker's radar is that, while researching the Secret Commonwealth's network, Abbey spots the LARP-master's name on an employee list at Enfortech, a firm that designs products used for non-lethal crowd control. (Think tear gas and Tasers, but weirder: net guns, acoustic cannons, and even some kind of prototype heat ray appears on their website.) What is the link between Langenderbach and all this exotic law enforcement hardware? Most of the movie consists of Abbey trying to figure out just that, and it leads him through a strange underground seldom perceived in urban North America.

And when I say "underground," I mean it almost literally. As we discover, the game uses an imaginary spatialization of the Lower Mainland into "realms"—each a fantasy turf over which the Secret Commonwealth players squabble, divided into warring factions with battles played out through Langenderbach's algorithm. These imaginary cantons are superimposed over the topography of real-life Vancouver and its outlying suburbs. (Looking at the website, I was somehow unfazed to find that my own East Vancouver neighbourhood, for example, is designated as a series of subterranean caverns called "the Shadow Realm.")

As Abbey gets closer to the game's creator, it becomes clear that Langenderbach is using his game design experience to create some sort of paramilitary device for Enfortech, and that he has used the Secret Commonwealth LARP to test-run the device. The Magister Ludi of this nutty scene turns out to be an exacting figure who created the Secret Commonwealth out of a small group of gamers and nerds, growing it into a thriving business with a massive online component. While it's too complex to describe here, the game is basically always running, and although the face-to-face meetings that players hold monthly during the spring and summer in parks and campgrounds are important, their movements online also extend play into a real-time, 24/7 digital experience—at home, at work, at school, always. The storylines that hold it all together are carefully crafted by Langenderbach behind the scenes, with players acting out their roles through various platforms—though how much control players have in influencing the plot seems unclear. The players, at least, believe they are co-creating their own epics, but to hear Langenderbach talk about it, he can and does manipulate the results he desires. Without spoiling the film's ending, I'll just say that after Abbey covertly films the use of holographic antagonists at a Secret Commonwealth campsite gathering, exactly what Langenderbach is up to in his side-career with Enfortech starts to become unnervingly clear. The interview that Abbey manages to finally arrange on camera is shocking yet interpretable in multiple ways.

The film's last surprise is Abbey's own skill. One appreciates the risks this debut takes. For example, the film concludes with a series of images that invoke the implicit parallels and paradoxes evident in documentary filmmaking, the nature of the camera, our attraction to secret societies, and the uncanny future of interactive holography. We circle back to the film-maker's own odd origins and, without making this all about him, Abbey manages to explain the appeal Langenderbach's world has for those who feel themselves to be outcasts and misfits, like himself. Although at first Abbey resisted partaking in the Secret Commonwealth, he explains how he came to feel enveloped in an atmosphere of acceptance, which he suggests remains the subculture's best feature. It's a place where weird is welcome. But how this translates into Langenderbach's worrisome laissez-faire ethos is not plainly spelled out. Abbey lets viewers process on their own whatever moral questions remain. No matter what one makes of it, the exposure of this otherwise unseen world reveals something about the nature of adult make-believe in the twenty-first century. In our time, this film seems to suggest, the pastoral innocence of play may always share an uneasy border with the castle-keep of force, security, and an armed peace.

Detail from *Expropriatus* by Suhaima Sylvester Martin

From "File # OS-25-4-0-0-1; File Title: Jane Doe 39's blue notepad; Special Committee Access: Pending Review"

IT WAS LIKE waking up. Then it was a matter of being alone among them.

No touching, no embracing.

Merely walking.

She finds the insurgent sitting on the beach, looking across the green or the blue or the grey or the black water.

They sit there together for a few days, watching the sun rise and overtake them and set. They watch the lights of the buildings over there blanket the shape of the land at night, and the mist rise off the water in the morning. The wind blows through them.

They know the language of encounter. The words have been waiting for them in the air.

Audio Link

More Episodes

Transcript

Radio Free Northwest

Title: "Death in Detention"

Producer: Ruben Jang
Host: Lina Bern
Transcript: Kaz Lovric-Nygaard

LB: Welcome to Radio Free Northwest. I'm Lina Bern, and for the next hour I'll be talking to Peter Hammond, a journalist with Unsaid Media, who has been covering the recent death of a young girl earlier this week at the controversial Pauline Johnson Island Special Detention Facility. While hospital officials say she died of complications related to asthma, the girl's death has prompted renewed criticism of the government's handling of the ICDP migrants and the policy known as the Burrard Inlet Solution. Stay with us as we discuss the potential repercussions of this tragedy and its implications for the future of the ICDP migrants and for immigration policy in Canada today.

[Theme music; fade out]

LB: Welcome, Peter.

PH: Thanks for having me.

LB: Before we get into a discussion about the death of this young girl, perhaps you can provide us with some of the background on Pauline Johnson Island and the Special Detention Facility there. Have there been any recent developments that may have led up to this tragedy?

PH: Well, that's hard to say. Since the creation of the facility, access to the island has been severely restricted to journalists—basically, limited to only a few officially planned junkets. I've been on two of these, most recently at the end of last year. How much we can take these tours at face-value is uncertain, but I'll tell you what I've seen. For starters, the conversion of the residential tower into detention housing is barely perceptible. It's only really when you enter the front door that you realize that you are in a prison, of sorts. That is, the lobby has been converted into a security centre, with closed-circuit monitoring, a guard posting, and so forth. But inside, they don't actually lock down the migrants. The circumstances of ICDP render most ordinary security measures pretty much moot.

LB: Can you talk about that a little bit? When you were there, did you actually witness the phenomenon?

PH: No, not directly. But on my last visit, while I was there, some of the officers were returning from a patrol across the island having just picked up someone who had gone missing from the building.

LB: So they had blinked out?

PH: Yes.

LB: And the guards were returning them to the facility? Were the migrants resisting at all?

PH: No, not at all. We still don't seem to know for sure whether or not the displacement is a deliberate act or something that just happens—or perhaps sometimes one and sometimes the other. But it wasn't, it seemed to me, treated as an escape attempt or any such thing. As far as I saw, they were simply rounded up and returned to the building and that was that. What I do know is that ICDP is being studied on the island, at the facility. They are working on these exact questions.

LB: When you say "they"—?

PH: The presence of teams of researchers on the island is definitely thick. In fact, it seemed to me that there were more scientists than guards, though we were not allowed to talk to them. I was curious myself to know if all of the scientific observers and researchers there were Canadian or if there were teams from other countries as well.

LB: Americans, you mean?

PH: Yes, from the States. I suspect so.

LB: Were the scientific teams running experiments on the migrants?

PH: I really can't say what they are doing. If so, I didn't see anything of that sort. But as I said, we were brought in there very deliberately on a particular day, so I have no way of knowing if anything I saw was business as usual. All I can really tell you about is the condition of the detention centre and how things appeared when we were there.

LB: And what were your observations in that regard?

PH: Well, the building itself is in good condition and the migrants that I met seemed to be healthy. As I was saying, there's no real point locking them in, so the inmates appear to have the free run of the building. There's a yard they are allowed access to, but in shifts. It's fenced in, but of course, due to the nature of ICDP, I got the sense it was routine to find migrants outside and on other parts of the island—hence the patrols. I was even told that on more than one occasion the entire group of migrants disappeared and reappeared outside the walls of the facility, and had to be escorted back in.

LB: Astonishing.

PH: Indeed. As you know, it's "Individual and Collective Displacement Phenomenon," so while these folks mostly seem to blink-out singly, they sometimes do so as a group, just as when they were first found on the *Ocean Star*.

LB: Right. Now, during their arrival two years ago, their displacement included, somehow, the ship they were on. The *Ocean Star* itself, with the migrants on board, blinked, as you say, in and out of place, as was captured on film and witnessed by many. Does it seem possible or likely that they might do the same with the building they are currently housed in? That is to say, might it be possible that they could somehow cause the building itself to move through space?

PH: I think that's one of the questions the research teams must be concerned about. The short answer is that I'm pretty sure they just don't know. This whole experience has been so improbable and baffling that it seems ridiculous to even guess at what the bounds of possibility are anymore. But, no, when they blink collectively, so far at least, it seems only to be in a kind of herding effect, for lack of a better term. They disappear from their various units and appear all together twenty metres or so beyond the walls of the building, standing in a crowd.

LB: Has there been any protest from the migrants on the island?

PH: I haven't heard of any sort of violence or disobedience. The original thinking behind the use of Pauline Johnson Island as a detention site seems to have been basically effective. As you'll recall, when the migrants were first apprehended, they were detained at the Burnaby Correctional Facility, but the ICDP effect meant that migrants kept disappearing and reappearing outside the prison. Because the migrants had been individually blinking in and out from the moment they landed, at what appeared to be random times and distances, a proper head count was impossible, so it's never been clear how many migrants initially arrived, and how many may in fact be at large. When the public understood that the migrants were uncontainable at the Burnaby Facility, well, that's when we got a bit of hysteria. There was a lot of pressure on the government to make sure they were locked down and not disappearing, one by one, into the general population. The logic behind the use of PJI is that the migrants never seemed to blink onto the ocean, even when the ship they were found on was at sea. When they disappear, they always seem to reappear on dry land, and never really at a greater distance than a kilometre or thereabouts. So detention on an island was considered the most viable way of securing them in one spot. And after the Global Acquisitions Crisis, the tower block on PJI had fallen into complete disuse, so the federal government bought the property and repurposed it. The Prime Minister and the coalition pushed the legislation through parliament. That's the short course on Bill C-77. Then Dave Schoen dubbed it "the Burrard Inlet Solution," and that name stuck.

LB: Right. And you believe it has so far been effective? No migrant has been able to disappear off the island?

PH: Well, that's what we're told. I can't be sure of it, but it does seem like the number of migrants on both of my own visits has been about the same.

LB: Do you have any thoughts on how long the migrants are likely to be detained there?

PH: Your guess is as good as mine. The other problem, of course, is that no one has yet determined the country of origin of the migrants, and it hasn't been possible to communicate with them in any substantial way. Their language has not been identified. I was told also that some of the researchers working there are in fact linguists trying to break this barrier. The language they speak is nothing anyone else seems to have heard before; nothing they had with them can be used to conclusively place their origins—no identification papers or anything like that was found on anyone in the entire group. Even if there was a plan to deport them, where would that be to? It's a stalemate.

LB: Now, the death of this girl—I'm sorry, but do we know her name? Reports say that it is unknown.

PH: They have given the migrants numbers until names can be ascertained. To be honest, I can't bring myself to use a number to speak of her.

LB: Understood. Tell us what you know about the night leading up to her death.

PH: The official report is that the girl had asthma, which was known previously. She had been treated for it.

LB: There is a medical staff at the facility?

PH: Yes.

LB: Go on.

PH: Well, at 2:47 a.m. on the morning of May 18th, the girl's parents brought her to the medical station. She was conscious but having serious trouble breathing. Staff treated her, but quickly decided that she needed to be evacuated. A helicopter was called in to take her to Vancouver. It landed on the roof of St. Paul's Hospital, which has a purpose-built helipad, at 3:18 a.m., and she was pronounced dead shortly thereafter. They say she was six years old.

LB: So sad.

PH: Yes, it is.

LB: Was she the youngest of the migrants?

PH: No. There are a few other children at the facility, some younger, some older. Also at least one of the incarcerated women is known to be currently pregnant. When they first apprehended the *Ocean Star*, the girl we're talking about was four. And apparently she had picked up some English from the guards and researchers. I don't know what her proficiency would have been like, and how practical it would be for such a young child to help in any way with translation, but I imagine that she must have been of great interest to all involved, being possibly the only English speaker among the group.

LB: Now some have been critical of the handling of this incident.

PH: Certainly. The amount of time it took for the girl to receive attention, the isolation of the facility—it's brought a degree of alarm and has put some pressure on the government to bring this to some kind of resolution.

LB: Do you think that's possible? What would a resolution look like?

PH: It's very hard to say. The best thing would be for this process to be as transparent as possible. However, the inaccessibility of the island itself makes that difficult. I don't feel like we really know what's going on there, or what the long-term plan is. But I will say that I have been there, I have seen these people up close, and can tell you that they are more ordinary than you might expect, given the strangeness of the circumstances. There is no reason to believe that they are fundamentally any different from the rest of us.

LB: Thank you, Peter. Would you be willing to answer some questions from the public on these issues?

PH: Sure. I'll do my best.

LB: After this short break, we'll go to the phones. Your calls next!

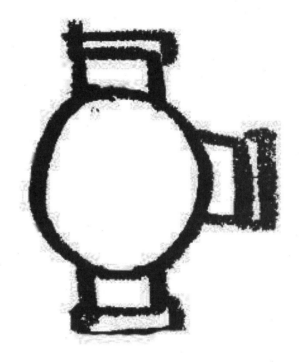

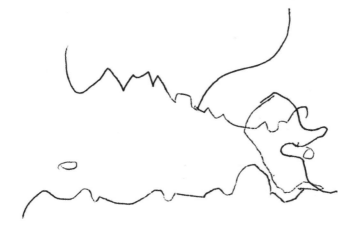

THE GIRL AND the insurgent sit beside each other on the sand. The waves attack the beach. On the horizon, the city burns. A scroll of smoke unfolds skyward out of a geometry of high-rises.

The insurgent remembers seeing a column of ash similarly rise from the centre of the island he now inhabits, remembers when he and his comrades were reconnoitering it, before his death. He is disoriented by the memory, and wonders for a moment where he really is.

You and me, she says.

He looks at her and she looks back. Sorrow and fear in her young eyes.

He offers his hand to her. The girl hesitates, looks down, looks away. Then she shifts a little closer. She finally reaches out and rests her palm in his.

She gazes at the city skyline. She knows something. It comes into her mind. She says, There's someone there we need to help.

Where?

She lifts her hand from his and points to the smouldering city across the water.

We can't.

We have to. It's one of us.

He looks at her, this dark-haired, dark-eyed child. One of who?

Us, she says. Like you and me.

He looks back at the city. Haze and helicopters. Sirens and fire.

We have to help, she repeats. We have to go there.

It's so empty here, the two of them alone. He imagines another.

Okay.

A small boat is there in the surf, a vessel made of black volcanic glass, chiselled out of their discourse. It will seat three easily. They board it, and the insurgent shoves off with one of its two gleaming oars. Then he slots them into their locks and rows to the smoke.

From "Experimental Crowd Control Methods and Advances
in Perceptual Manipulation" by P.W. Haarman

"The concern of this report is the viability of a pacification tool—the Multiple Perception Immobilization Device
(MPID)—developed in the private sector by the Canadian
company Waking Dream Entertainment Services. Waking
Dream has crossed over from primarily marketing multime-
dia 'live action role-playing' supplies to providing security
solutions for law enforcement and military purposes after
being acquired by Enfortech early last year.

"The basic concept of the MPID was developed by Waking
Dream's founder and CEO, Jamie Langenderbach, whose
team pioneered systems of live gaming involving holographic 'crowd-seeding'—that is, an effect in which a player
in the middle of an open space can be made to perceive
a human figure standing or walking near him or her, in
all appearances to the eye seeming real and three-dimensional. The original scenarios for the project involved fantasy
gaming genres.

"It was, according to Langenderbach, when an early prototype of the MPID was activated during a late-night session,
and he noted a janitor's response to the sudden 'crowd' of
holograms in the room, that he first appreciated the system's
possible weaponization. Though the holograms are completely immaterial and can be walked through, Langenderbach
noticed that the janitor, who did not realize the room was
filled only with projections, froze and attempted to move
through the 'crowd' without touching the figures around him.
Langenderbach says that the inspiration to adapt this effect

to crowd control was also directly inspired by his experience of witnessing first-hand the Vancouver hockey riot of 2011.

"The tactical device works in the following manner: the MPID projects holographic images of people into a crowd, causing a perceived doubling or tripling of the crowd density, in turn causing rioting individuals to perceive themselves as surrounded by a far denser crowd than is the actual case. The device initially scans the suspects, making composite holograms by recombining facial features, clothing, etc. so that its seeded projections closely resemble the demographics of the targeted crowd.

"The beauty of the MPID for crowd control is that it does not intensify the perception of threat to the crowd, and thereby does not cause further instigation of anti-social behaviour. Rather, the effect causes the instinctive immobilization and/ or slowing of subjects, who believe their movements are restricted. By inflating their numbers artificially, the rioters become distracted, slowed, and ultimately vulnerable to other pacification measures. The MPID comes with hologram-cancelling goggles that may be worn by enforcement agents and observers, enabling them to intervene unimpeded into a 'crowd-seeded' zone in order to arrest or disable suspects.

"While the MPID has yet to be used in a domestic situation, it has been previewed overseas, though details on those outcomes are currently unavailable."

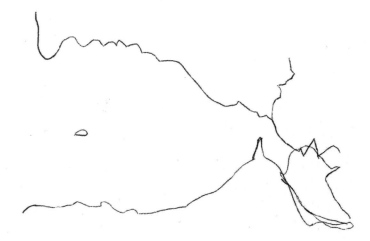

HE PLUNGES THE blades into the water and leans back, his weight levering the boat through the bay. He leans forward, then leans back, then does it again.

He faces the island they died on, as he moves the boat away from it.

She sits at the stern, now and then directing him, watching the shore come slowly closer. The city is veiled in smoke and tear gas. As they approach the shore, she sees the figure on the beach.

Waiting.

For them.

The insurgent brings them as close as he can without grounding the hull, then puts up the oars. He turns around and looks.

The composite is wearing black, has short dark hair unmoved by the wind.

Is that—? The insurgent is uncertain of what to say—him or her.

They need us, the girl says. She stands and the boat rocks. She puts out her hand, gesturing. Come, she says. Come with us.

The composite hesitates. They watch carefully, thinking. Then the composite looks back at the city, turns away from it, steps finally into the water, takes the girl's hand, boards.

When the three of them are settled in the boat, the insurgent works one oar in the chuck until they are turned around, and he begins the labour of going back.

Blades in the air. Blades in the water. Forward and back.

His body makes a hinge.

From "Counter Clockwise and the G25 Riots: Fighting
Fabulism with Fabulism?" by Versajna

"In the months leading up to the recent G25 Summit in
Vancouver, a group of performance artists came together to
form a collective called Counter Clockwise. The group was
formed in order to conceptually examine what has become
a grotesque *pas de deux* of the long twenty-first century: the
governing heads of state conspire regularly to meet in the
form of G7, G8, G20, and now G25 summits, and the people
answer back by attempting to disrupt their meetings by all
means possible.

"The members of Counter Clockwise did not come together
with any strongly developed critique of this political tradition.
But we wondered if the responsive pattern—they act and we
answer—might be limiting our thinking and our appreciation
of the scope and scale of the problem. Initially we were merely
seeking to estrange a pattern that seemed too rote, as artists
are wont to do. The political implications, we believed, would
follow from there.

"Our idea was to stage a *pre-enactment* of the G25 riot we
all assumed would happen. We decided we would pantomime,
as it were, the riot we expected, one whole month *before* the
start of the summit. We choreographed a group of performers
to act out our imagined civil disorder on the streets of downtown Vancouver, as a fore-echo of the real thing we believed
would likely come.

"As it turned out, and as we are all well aware, a large-
scale riot did in fact occur later, during the summit—leading
to the largest mass arrest in Canadian history and upward

of $20 million worth of property damage. Scores of people were injured, at least one critically, and there are currently 718 people with charges before the court.

"The most obvious difference between our pre-enactment and the actual riot is the size of each. We used fifty actors in total, divided into one group of fifteen mock-police and thirty-five mock-rioters. As a site, we chose Canada Place at the foot of Howe Street, near the primary site of the scheduled summit—the Pan Pacific Hotel and the adjoining convention centre. Our group occupied the street on a busy Saturday afternoon and quickly formed two groups: a line of uniform-clad, baton-wielding, shield-thumping 'police'—though we were careful to use only generic, unmarked uniforms to avoid charges of impersonation; and a crowd of 'protestors' with banners and placards, who immediately began throwing papier-mâché bricks and bottles at the 'cops.' The performance of the skirmish lasted about ten minutes, after which all the participants shed their costumes, dropped their props, and left in different directions to avoid being ticketed or arrested.

"In stark contrast, the real G25 riot was massive and prolonged, covering most of downtown Vancouver, with incidents at all of the G25 meeting sites, in some cases over a kilometre apart—Canada Place, the Queen Elizabeth Theatre, the Wall Centre, and the Hotel Vancouver. It lasted for nearly nine hours on Friday, with a partial resurgence the following day. Unlike our pre-enactment, *real* bottles, bricks, and batons were used, and fires were set at three banks. But the most surprising and bizarre weapon used was a new non-lethal crowd-control device called the Multiple Perception Immobilization Device (or the MPID), which was employed at the Wall Centre during the height of the fighting there. As this is the first time the device has been used for crowd control in Canada, I want to discuss our experience in detail, as several members of Counter Clockwise, including myself, were there, and experienced its effects directly.

"It is important to note the chronology of events that after-noon: the protests on Burrard Street, a block away from the Wall Centre, which was sectioned off behind a series of rein-forced fences, had taken an angry turn when the information reached us that the police had shot and killed a protestor at the Hotel Vancouver just a few blocks north. While it was later clarified that the victim, Jue Ma, a postdoctoral international student who was participating in the demonstration, had been shot by a plastic bullet, resulting in a cracked rib and perfo-rated lung, the rumour on the street was that the police had fired *live* rounds at unarmed demonstrators, killing at least one. (In fact, although Ma was seriously injured, he ultimately recovered.) But when the group at the Wall Centre broke away and started moving north along Burrard, in the direction of the shooting, the police decided to use the MPID to stop us. Riot police on the ground at the Hotel Vancouver were at that moment attempting to evacuate Ma, whom they had appre-hended after he went down, in the face of a crowd made increasingly hostile by this use of force. Anticipating our con-tingent's addition to that situation surely caused a degree of panic in the ranks of the police, and we believe led to the use of the MPID device.

"The MPID was employed as our group was passing north-bound on Burrard through the intersection at Nelson. The effect was immediate. Although we did not realize it, several cameras, as part of the MPID, had been scanning the demonstrators, creating composite images digitally stitched together out of our randomized features, and loading them into the device's projectors. In an instant, the crowd moving through the intersection appeared to triple in numbers, and I can attest that it was impossible on the ground to discern the three-dimensional holographic 'bodies' around me from those of my real companions. I did not see where the projections were coming from, though people later reported that projectors were spotted on nearby rooftops, aimed down at us.

"The operators of the MPID were apparently programming the holograms to either stand still or walk in the reverse direction the crowd was originally moving, clearly intending to confuse our progress north, and to ultimately cause us to halt. It worked. The effect was like standing in the middle of a sea of people, and though I could pass through the holograms, and we realized projections were being used, the realism of the imagery was enough to make me hesitate significantly, and after colliding with more than one person I'd taken for fake, I moved more slowly and uncertainly, which is the machine's intended function.

"But by far the strangest moment was when I noticed a particular hologram that I am certain was created out of a combination of my own features with that of my partner and fellow Counter Clockwise member, Riel Graham, who was there with me at the demonstration. I saw a particular 'person' in the crowd and immediately felt a sense of recognition, seeing some of my own facial features as it passed; but in its face I also saw Riel's—his eyes, my brow, his cheekbones, my chin, and our clothes patchworked into one outfit. It was transfixing.

Our holographic 'child' (as I think of it now) was walking in the opposite direction, south on Burrard, away from our destination, moving, it seemed to me, with purpose. I eventually lost sight of it in the crowd.

"After the program ran for perhaps ten minutes, I realized the riot police had intervened, each wearing the special goggles that cancel the effects of the holograms. As confused and disoriented as people were, it was not difficult for them to arrest particular targets and disperse the rest of us with violent force, charging some with shields and hitting others with batons, as they pleased. We managed to flee west on Nelson, though our bloc was effectively broken, with multiple arrests and injuries.

"What are the lessons learned? What is the result of the initial experiment and performance in light of the events that followed? It is difficult to say. But it is hard not to notice that we appear to have entered a moment in which the weapons and tactics on both sides seem to be verging into phantasm, simulation, and fable. Perhaps this is only logical—the economic crisis that was the subject of the summit itself and the source of the anger that led to these riots is, like each crisis that preceded it, a matter of illusion failing in the light of verisimilitude. As we stare down each impending collapse, their only answer is that the show must go on. So how might we get around, above, or outside it? What is the way forward?

"Counter Clockwise was our best shot this time to edge closer to some sort of answer, as inadequate as our efforts ultimately were. We can't tell what the future holds, but it will surely include a protracted campaign of clashing imaginations."

THE GIRL AND the composite are quiet as the insurgent rows. He guides them away from Sunset Beach and through English Bay, to the most open waters of the harbour.

When their island is in sight, the composite disappears then reappears. The girl notices, and looks at the insurgent, worry on her face. It happens again, a strobing or flickering of the composite's form. The insurgent stops rowing, puts the black oars up.

The composite looks at the girl, then looks at the rower, all the while being there, not there, being there. An expression of terror.

The insurgent says to the girl, Are they like you?

How do you mean?

Blinking, he says.

She looks at the composite, going in and out of presence, breaking up.

No, she says. The projectors.

He looks at where they've come from. We're out of range. It's amazing we've made it this far.

They drift for a while, the composite going on and off, exchanging glances with both of them. Finally the composite says in a fracturing voice, Ke. ep go. ing.

The insurgent considers this. The girl looks at him, her eyes pleading, No, filling with water. He looks away from her.

Ple. ase.

The insurgent regards the city from the drifting boat. It goes up and down with the swells, and the composite goes on and off through the play of some fantastic wave of light. The tether will eventually break, whatever he does.

He sets the blades in the water.

Pulls. Lifts.

Leans. Sets.

Pulls again.

The composite shudders once more, then is gone.

The insurgent keeps rowing.

The girl sobs.

She screams at him to turn the boat around. But he keeps going.

He works till they close in on the island. He remembers the last time he approached this place in that other boat, and the memory suffuses him. He rows the vessel in, till the oars touch the bottom and he can go no more.

He stands, then jumps into the surf. Offers his hand to the girl. She rubs her eyes and lets him steady her disembarkation into the knee-deep water. He'll let the boat drift away. But just before they abandon it, they see: the composite is sitting inside, at the bow.

The girl smiles and splashes through the water, reaches, embraces. The composite, with her help, steps over the hull and into the tide with them. No more flickering. Dead. There. The three walk through the waves until they reach dry land. They stop and survey their progress.

The composite wants to walk around, see all of this place. The girl is excited to be a knowing guide and takes the composite by the hand, to show the detention centre, the research facilities, the other shores, her parents, the people who can't perceive them. But the insurgent stays behind at the landing site. He has memories to sort through, brought up by the boat, the journey, and all its echoes. He looks out there, feeling them.

At dawn, he and she and the newcomer will make plans to rendezvous with those yet to come. They will discuss what it means to regroup.

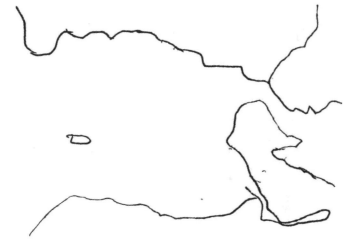

ACKNOWLEDGMENTS

Thanks to Anne Stone, my first reader, who helped immensely in bringing better versions of these stories forward. Thanks to the following people and groups who contributed directly or indirectly to the development of this book: Hari Alluri; Elizabeth Bachinsky and the editors at *Event*; Jonathan Chen; Andrew Chesham; la Coalition large de l'Association pour une Solidarité Syndicale Étudiante (CLASSE); Jason de Couto; Jen Currin, whose poem "A Human Place I Visited Recently While Traveling from Wind to Light" scored the composition of the last half of this project; Stan Douglas and Michael Turner for *Journey into Fear* (2001); Leslie Hill; the Hogan's Alley Memorial Project; Mat Johnson, Tayari Jones, and the 2007 *Callaloo* fiction cohort at Texas A&M; No One Is Illegal (Vancouver); Occupy Vancouver; Chandra Prasad; Renée Sarojini Saklikar; R. Murray Schafer; Danzy Senna; Betsy Warland and everyone in the Writer's Studio at Simon Fraser University Continuing Studies—in particular my 2006 Non-Fiction students, who generously responded to the earliest of these stories; and Jennifer Zilm.

I am particularly grateful to those who contributed their visual art to the creation of this book: Diyan Achjadi, for allowing us to use a detail from "Merapi" (2007) for the cover; April Milne,

for her illustrations in "The Boom" and "The Outer Harbour";
Roger Hur, for his photograph in "The Outer Harbour"; and
my daughter, Senna Stone Compton, who is five years old, for
her maps of Vancouver as seen by the migrant ghost girl in
the story "The Outer Harbour." The poster "Justice for Fletcher
Sylvester" in the story "The Boom" includes an adaptation of
a photograph of Surtsey Island by Worldtraveller (CC BY-SA
3.0), and the poster "Demonstration Against the Rezoning
of Pauline Johnson Island" incorporates a photograph of a
microphone by Chris Engelsma (CC BY-SA 3.0).

Thanks to the whole crew at Arsenal Pulp Press—Brian Lam,
Robert Ballantyne, Cynara Geissler, Gerilee McBride, and
Susan Safyan—wonderful people, all; Susan's editing strength-
ened the project enormously as a unified whole.

I would like to thank the Canada Council for the Arts, the
British Columbia Arts Council, the Simon Fraser University
Ellen & Warren Tallman Writer in Residence Program, and the
Vancouver Public Library's Writer in Residence Program for
material support that made it possible for me to devote time
to writing these stories.

WAYDE COMPTON is the author of *49th Parallel Psalm* (a finalist for the Dorothy Livesay Poetry Prize), *Performance Bond,* and *After Canaan: Essays on Race, Writing, and Region* (nominated for the City of Vancouver Book Award). He also edited *Bluesprint: Black British Columbian Literature and Orature.* Compton is the program director of Creative Writing at Simon Fraser University Continuing Studies. He lives in Vancouver. *waydecompton.com*